Roommate Wanted

"Are you Alison Parker?" he asked.

How did he know her name? "Who are you?" she asked.

"Billy Campbell," he said, holding out his hand like he was a politician asking for her vote. Realizing her arms were full of groceries, he dropped his hand. "I'm a friend of Natalie's."

"Then I feel sorry for you," Alison said, heading for the door. "Natalie doesn't live here any more." Billy followed her.

"Yeah, well, that's why I'm here, because Natalie told me she was moving," he said. Further proof that Natalie Miller was a miserable excuse for a human being, Alison thought, telling her friends, but not her roommate that she was moving. Alison would have told the boy so if he'd let her get a word in edgewise.

Don't miss these other books in the exciting
MELROSE PLACE series

MELROSE PLACE Off the Record

And coming soon

MELROSE PLACE Keeping the Faith

Published by
HarperPaperbacks

BASED ON THE TELEVISION SERIES
CREATED BY DARREN STAR

MELROSE PLACE
© Spelling Television Inc.

TOUGH LOVE

A NOVELIZATION BY DEAN JAMES
FROM TELEPLAYS BY FREDERICK
RAPPAPORT, CHARLES PRATT, JR., AND
DARREN STAR

HarperPaperbacks
A Division of HarperCollinsPublishers

HarperPaperbacks *A Division of* HarperCollins*Publishers*
10 East 53rd Street, New York, N.Y. 10022

Cover and insert photos by Andrew Semel

First Printing: December 1992

Printed in the United States of America

HarperPaperbacks and colophon are trademarks of HarperCollins*Publishers*

❖ 10 9 8 7 6 5 4 3 2 1

1

IT WAS JUST ANOTHER CRIME IN THE
night, in a city that has more than its share of
crimes in the night, a minor betrayal and nothing
personal—just the way things went sometimes. The
city was Los Angeles, 4616 Melrose Place, to be
specific, the event marked by the sound of footsteps
echoing in a faux-Spanish courtyard full of potted
palmettos and colored lights, while above, a pair of
eyes bore silent witness through Venetian blinds.

A woman set her suitcases down momentarily
to rip the name "Miller" off a mailbox. She was
young and attractive, but it didn't really matter
because in L.A., everybody was young and attractive, which made it easy to disappear into the

crowd. She picked up her belongings, took one last furtive glance over her shoulder, and made her escape.

A few hours later, a clock radio went off in Apartment Three. A sunny-voiced announcer announced another sunny day in LaLa Land, "present temperature seventy-two, air-quality unhealthful . . ."

Alison Parker awoke from a dream of Midwestern dairy farms and pine trees to look at the clock. It was seven-thirty. Alison was also young and attractive, in an admittedly wholesome sort of way, but the only crowd she disappeared into each day was the labor force. Beyond the window, palm trees swayed under unhealthful blue skies. Palm trees. They still seemed fake to her, but then, she thought, in L.A., just because something is real doesn't mean it isn't fake, too.

"Natalie?" Alison called out, stumbling down the hall, still half asleep. "Your turn to make the coffee. Nat?" She passed the bathroom to knock on her roommate's door, which she found half open. She opened it all the way, to find a stripped mattress, an empty chest of drawers and an empty closet. Still not quite fully awake, it took her a moment for it all to sink in. "Dammit!"

With a grim expression, she raced downstairs and knocked on Matt Fielding's apartment door. Matt answered the door in his bathrobe his disheveled appearance making him seem younger than his early twenties. He took one look at Alison, in her own terry cloth robe, and asked if she was out of coffee again.

"Natalie's gone," Alison said. "She and all her things have disappeared." Matt looked concerned. He was the kind of guy you could always count on to be concerned, the kind of guy people confided in. "Did you know anything about this, Matt?"

"Nothing, I swear," he said. She also knew she could believe him. "Maybe she's been kidnapped?"

"Come on, Matt—who would want Natalie?"

"Space aliens," he dead-panned. She glared at him. "You read about it all the time."

"Thanks for your help," she replied.

At the next apartment over, Alison knocked hard on the door. The door was opened by an incredibly handsome well-built man wearing only boxer shorts. Ordinarily Alison might have enjoyed seeing an incredibly handsome well-built man wearing only boxer shorts open a door, any door, but she was in no mood. Jake Hanson was not a morning person, and ran his fingers through his hair groggily.

"Jake, have you seen Natalie?" Alison asked.

"Natalie?" he said, still in a fog.

"My roommate," Alison said, casting a suspicious glance over Jake's shoulder. "Is she in there?"

"Why is it every time a girl doesn't come home at night, people think she's in my apartment?" he asked.

Because half the time, Alison wanted to say, they'd be right. "Well is she?"

"No."

Only Michael and Jane could save her now.

In Apartment Five, Jane Mancini was making

her best move on her husband, Michael, kissing him on the cheek, the neck, a gentle nuzzle behind the ear. In his dream, Michael was a young and handsome over-worked medical student who carried the weight of the world on his shoulders. Unfortunately, in real life, Michael was also a young and handsome over-worked medical student who carried the weight of the world on his shoulders.

"Honey, please," he said, turning away. "I was making rounds until three in the morning. Can't you let me sleep?"

"So sleep," Jane said, continuing to kiss him. Sometimes she worried that she was losing her touch. Other times she worried she was losing Michael's touch. This time she saw the corners of his mouth turn up and knew she had him. He sighed with pleasure.

"I'll give you exactly one hour to stop that," he said, turning to face her and grinning. A loud knock on the door interrupted.

They froze. He whispered to her, "Maybe if we don't make a sound, the problem will go away."

"Michael," Jane chastised. She remembered the days when they would have pulled the covers over their heads and hid, but they were married now, and with marriage came maturity. With maturity came responsibility, including jobs like being apartment managers in exchange for free rent. Jane threw back the sheets and headed for the door.

It was Alison, standing with her arms wrapped tightly around her chest.

"Don't tell me," Jane said. "It's the plumbing."

Milt —

7-23-93

I couldn't resist this
book — hopefully it'll
tide you over until next
season starts! (just kidding)
I'm waiting for "Central
Park West," the new series!

Take Care,
Molly

"No. Natalie ditched me."

"She ditched you? What do you mean?"

"She took off during the night and stuck me with the rent."

"Are you sure?"

"She never said anything to you, did she?" Alison asked. Michael appeared at Jane's shoulder, looking grumpy in an early morning way. He assumed it was the plumbing, until Jane told him what had happened. Alison asked him if it was possible for her to pay only half her rent that month. She had a hunch what the answer would be.

"I don't think so," Michael said. "Was Natalie's name on the lease?" Alison shook her head. "Bad move."

"Can you stall the landlord a few days for me?" Alison begged. "Just until I find another roommate?" Michael looked at her as if she were a fourth grader, telling the teacher the dog ate her homework.

"Alison," he said. "This is real life. You can't just stall on the rent."

"Look," she pleaded, "I finally found a job out here after three months, my savings are wiped out, I'm living on Cup-a-Soup until I get my first paycheck in two weeks—I just don't have it." Michael's face was a stone mask. "This has got to be the worst thing that ever happened to me."

"Then maybe you need to spend a night with me at the L.A. County Emergency Room and learn some lessons about real human suffering . . ."

"Michael—" Jane interrupted.

"Forget it," Alison said. "He's right. I'm an

adult and I'm going to deal with it. I'll just have to find a new roommate." She felt like she was going to cry. "I'll deal with it. Somehow."

The walls were thin at Melrose Place, and as Jane closed the door, Alison could hear Jane telling Michael he'd been mean. "What do you want me to do?" Alison heard him reply, "loan her money we don't have? Maybe we can get evicted and she can stay?" Some people thought Michael and Jane had the ideal marriage, but Alison suspected the stress of his long hours and managing the apartment was getting to them. Right now though, she had her own problems.

She was heading back to her own empty apartment when she saw Rhonda approaching. Rhonda Blair was a bit older, about thirty, black and gorgeous, an aerobics instructor with about as much fat on her as a number two pencil. She was wearing leotards and carrying her dance bag.

"I got to run," Rhonda said, "I teach cardio-funk in ten minutes, but girlfriend, I saw the whole thing." Alison stopped dead. "The witch snuck out of here like a cat-burglar, around five in the morning. Stuck you with the rent and a bunch of bills—am I right?" Alison nodded. "I knew that's what she was doing when I saw her dragging her suitcases out of here."

"Why didn't you stop her?" Alison said.

Rhonda shrugged. "I couldn't—it was none of my business.

"I don't understand it," Alison said. It was getting late and she knew she should be getting dressed. "We lived together for three months. I thought she was my friend."

"Well I never trusted her," Rhonda said. "She kept promising to take my class. 'I'll be there Rhonda, I promise.' Ha!"

"I don't know what I'm going to do," Alison said with exasperation. "If I don't find a roommate in two days, I'll be sleeping in my car." Assuming nobody stole her car first.

"Put an ad in the paper," Rhonda advised. "There are thousands of new people coming into town every day. Just don't be too picky. How do you think I ended up living with Sandy?" Rhonda's roommate was a debutant/femme-fatale/actress/waitress, a blonde-bombshell with a heart of coal. Other than that, she wasn't so bad. Rhonda winked and headed out of the courtyard, leaving Alison to deal with her dilemma.

Driving to work, Alison realized living in her car wouldn't require as much of a transition as she thought—she already spent hours a day in bumper-to-bumper freeway traffic. Ahead of her meek little Honda with Wisconsin plates was a cream-colored Rolls-Royce with NBDY U KNW vanity plates. Behind her, a forty-year-old beat-up Chevy pick-up with a family's belongings roped in back as if they'd driven straight out of the pages of *Grapes of Wrath*. Alison tried to decide how to word her ad. "DOWN-TO-EARTH FEMALE, PROFESSIONAL, 23, FUN AND NEAT, SEEKS OTHER NON-SMOKING DRUG-FREE CAREER-

ORIENTED ENVIRONMENTALLY CONSCIOUS *RESPONSIBLE* FEMALE UNDER 30 TO SHARE 2 BDRM APT IN HOLLYWOOD, $400/MO REFERENCES A MUST." It made her sound too elitist—you didn't want to limit your options too much. "FEMALE 23, FUN AND NEAT, SEEKS OTHER NON-SMOKING ENVIRONMENTALLY CONSCIOUS RESPONSIBLE FEMALE UNDER 35 TO SHARE . . ." That made her sound a little too earth-mother-peasant-skirts-Birkenstocks-wool-socks-and-hairy-legs. "FEMALE SEEKS NON-SMOKING ROOMMATE, ANY AGE, TO SHARE . . ." Traffic began to move again. "God, I'm desperate," she said out loud.

She was thinking how things couldn't possibly get any worse as she parked her car in the lot at D&D Advertising. She opened her door wide and heard a thunk. A definite thunk. The kind you hear when you open your car door and hit the passenger door of the car parked next to you. Exactly that kind of thunk. She closed her eyes. Please let it be a pick-up truck from the *Grapes of Wrath*, she prayed. She opened her eyes. It was not. It was a black BMW. It was her boss's black BMW. And he was standing right there. Hal Barber was handsome, late thirties, well-tailored and, from the look on his face, incredibly pissed off.

"Oh, God I'm sorry, I didn't see you," Alison said, getting out of her car and eying the damage. She smiled weakly. "It's just a ding."

"There's no such thing as 'just a ding' with this car—it'll probably cost a grand to repair," he said, touching the mark Alison had left with his finger. He looked at her. "Don't I know you?"

If she couldn't even pay the rent, she certainly didn't have a thousand dollars to fix his car, and she didn't dare tell him that, times being thin of late, she'd had to temporarily let her insurance lapse. She wondered if L.A. had debtor's prisons? Alison considered giving him a fake name, Carmen Miranda, maybe, or better yet, Natalie Miller. Instead she gave her own, and admitted that she was the new receptionist, holding out her hand.

He shook it. Something about the way he shook it seemed to say, don't worry, I'm insured, but that might have been wishful thinking on her part.

"Hal Barber," he said. They walked into the building together. "So you're the new receptionist."

"That's me," Alison said, surmising that now wouldn't be a bad time to kiss butt. "I've seen your name on a lot of great ad campaigns. I hope I can be as good as you some day." He looked her over, probably trying to decide whether to fire her on the spot or drag it out for fun. "We haven't met but I've put calls through to your office."

"None from my wife, I hope," he said as they reached the lobby where Alison worked. She shrugged to say she didn't know. "I only say that because we're divorced. She got the house, I got the car." He smiled at her for the first time. "Be seeing you."

"Sorry about the car," Alison called after him, telephones ringing all around her. A reassuring "don't worry about it" would have been nice, but none was forthcoming. It was definitely not her day.

Back at Melrose Place, it wasn't Kelly Taylor's day either. She'd just dropped her step brother David and their friend Donna off at Johnny Rocket's, a hamburger joint on Melrose Avenue. It had been her idea to go there, but only because it was around the corner from 4616, where Jake lived.

All her friends were trying to warn her to stay away from Jake, telling her he was too old for her (a mere seven or eight years or so—half the couples at the Beverly Hills Beach Club were at least that far apart in age) or that the fact that he hadn't returned any of her many calls meant something. Usually Kelly tried to listen to her friends, but in this case, they didn't know what Kelly knew, and what Kelly knew was what Jake had told her, with his eyes, with his touch. What if something had happened to him? After what they'd shared the night of her mother's wedding, Kelly knew Jake would never blow her off without an explanation, and she didn't care what her friends said.

She found her way into the courtyard and was circling the pool when she noticed a woman in a reclining lawn chair. The woman was older than Kelly, mid-twenties and gorgeous, naturally blond, with a perfect body in a bathing suit that made the *Sports Illustrated* models look like a bunch of frumpy meter maids. She appeared to be sleeping behind her sunglasses. Kelly knocked on the door to

Jake's apartment.

"He's not home," the blonde called out not bothering to turn around.

Kelly felt disappointed and awkward, backing away from the door. She approached the woman by the pool. "Well," Kelly said, "could you just tell him that Kelly stopped by to say hello?" The woman removed her sunglasses to get a better look, looking Kelly up and down. Kelly felt the need to explain. "Jake did some work on my mom's house. We got to know each other pretty well."

The blonde just smirked.

"I see," she said, sounding intrigued. "And what do you do, Kelly?" She had a southern accent, genteel but so thick it almost seemed fake. Kelly didn't want to look like any more of a fool than she had to, but she wasn't sure what to say.

"I'm in school."

"College?"

"High school," Kelly admitted.

The blonde smiled again. "High school," the woman repeated. "And you're a friend of Jake's. Well, I'll be sure to tell him you stopped by."

As Kelly walked away, Sandy Harling slipped her glasses back on and smiled knowingly. Poor kid, she thought as she adjusted the towel beneath her legs.

Sandy was an aspiring actress, which, in Hollywood, are a dime a dozen, but she knew she was going to make it somehow. She was equally aware that in Hollywood, aspiring-actresses-who-know-they'll-make-it-somehow are also a dime a dozen, but all she could do was try.

She was what some people called a "southern belle," or as her grandfather might have said, a "soiled dove," a former first runner-up in the Miss South Carolina pageant. She'd have won but for her bad attitude, her mother had told her. Sandy Louise Harling came from a wealthy Charleston family, but they'd disowned her when she said she was moving to Hollywood (a marriage to the son of another wealthy Charleston family had been virtually arranged for her). So, to make ends meet, she was waiting tables at a bar called Shooters, not far from where she lived. It was a way to get by, for now. She lived in the now, and tried not to worry too much about the future.

At Shooters that night, Sandy found Jake sitting at his usual table, drinking his usual drink, beer; preoccupied with his usual preoccupation, girls. In this case a brunette he was flirting with from across the room. Women found Jake irresistible, a fact Sandy knew first hand. Later the women found their hearts broken, something Sandy also knew firsthand. She slammed a beer down on Jake's table to get his attention.

"Before you start flirting with every woman in here, maybe you should worry about the little high school girl who's been hanging around your apartment, waiting for you to turn up," Sandy suggested. It surprised her how mad she was, but then, for the most part, she liked being mad. Jake looked at her as if he didn't know what she was talking about. "Let me see, was it Kimberly? Katie . . . ?"

"Kelly," Jake said, still looking at the brunette. Shooters was a spacious but unpretentious neighborhood kind of bar/pool hall, where trendy Mickey Rourke types could shoot nine-ball for dollars with untrendy Charles Kuralt types, but not so quiet a place that you couldn't yell at somebody in private.

"That's it," Sandy said, "Kelly. Cute, blond hair, big weepy eyes—she's not even eighteen, Jake. How could you?"

"I didn't," he said. "Listen."

"Jake," Sandy interrupted, "you're a smart man, I really do believe it, but where women are concerned, you're totally off base. Don't tell me I'm wrong, I have firsthand experience, remember?"

"I remember," he said, smiling. The problem was that when Jake smiled, it was hard to maintain a useful level of outrage. When he smiled, you could see past the motorcycle and the leather jacket and tell there was someone good and kind inside, never mind the good looks. As for Jake's looks, the only man who'd ever put more butterflies in women's stomachs, Sandy thought, was Otis, as in Otis Elevators.

"One week after I moved in, you were romancing me so hard it turned me inside out," she told him. "The next week I hurt so bad from being dumped my body ached. Which would have been fine for both of us, if we never had to see each other again . . . it slip your mind that I lived next door?"

"Whatever happened to 'love thy neighbor?'" he joked.

"Cute, Jake. I can laugh now because I'm over it," she told him. "That girl this morning wasn't laughing. She's got some serious feelings for you. Sooner or later she's going to catch you at home and you're going to have to deal with it. Actions have consequences, Jake." She swung her hair off her shoulder as she strode away, not bothering to look back.

Alison Parker was still dealing with the consequences of her roommate's actions that night when she got home from work. She'd stopped at the grocery store first, where she'd swallowed her pride and bought enough Hamburger Helper to last a week. She hoped swallowing Hamburger Helper would be easier. Tiredly, she began unloading the groceries from her car.

"Hello."

Alison jumped aside, surprised to see a young man standing there behind her, a slip of paper in his hand.

"Oh," she said, backing away, still apprehensive. "You startled me." Somehow though, just judging him by his body language, he seemed too earnest and sincere to be a mugger.

"Are you Alison Parker?" he asked.

How did he know her name? "Who are you?" she asked.

"Billy Campbell," he said, holding out his hand

like he was a politician asking for her vote. Realizing her arms were full of groceries, he dropped his hand. "I'm a friend of Natalie's."

"Then I feel sorry for you," Alison said, heading for the door. "Natalie doesn't live here any more." Billy followed her.

"Yeah, well, that's why I'm here, because Natalie told me she was moving," he said. Further proof that Natalie Miller was a miserable excuse for a human being, Alison thought, telling her friends, but not her roommate that she was moving. Alison would have told the boy so if he'd let her get a word in edgewise.

"I was shooting pool at the bar down the street," he continued, "and I was telling this buddy of mine I gotta move out of my parents' place because it's been twenty-two years right through college and everybody has had it up to here, but with my insurance premiums it's either live with the 'rents and have a car or get an apartment and take the bus, both of which are heinous propositions in this town, because like, how would I date anybody? Because you can't pick someone up in a bus, but even keeping the car, what am I going to do—take her back to my folks' house and make out on the same twin bed that used to have Kermit the Frog bedsheets when I was little . . ."

"Have you got a point to make?" Alison said patiently, as she opened her apartment door, making sure he didn't try to follow her in.

"The point is, I can't date," Billy said. "I'm turning into this totally sexually repressed newt, the

way things are. So that night I'm telling my friend
I'm shooting pool with all this and this person
Natalie, who I've never met, overhears and tells me
she knows of a place that's going to be vacant in a
week, so she told me about you and your doll collection and your claustrophobia and how you yelp
in your sleep—"

"She told you all this?" Alison said in disbelief.
This guy was a complete stranger. He was getting
stranger all the time.

"Whatever," he said. "Anyway, I thought,
here's a place I can afford, with a girl roommate,
platonic of course—"

"Look," Alison said, not waiting for him to
stop talking. "I don't know who you are or what
this is about, but if you think for one minute I'm
going to live with some strange guy who turns up
on my doorstep talking about . . . Kermit the Frog
sheets and . . . and if Natalie Miller is your only ref-
erence, forget it, Bud." He stood looking at her,
waiting. He was kind of cute. Not that it mattered.

"Can I at least see the place?" he said, glancing
over her shoulder. "I might fall in love with it."

"No!" she said. What was with this guy? You
had to admire his temerity, but only to a point.
"Just go away."

"Okay," he said with a shrug. "You're uptight
and overly judgmental anyway. I get enough of that
from my mother."

"I am not," she said.

"Here's my number if you change your mind,"
he said, writing it on a matchbook advertising a

school that taught people to drive semi-tractor trailer trucks.

"Don't count on it," she told him as he left.

Once he was gone, she considered keeping the matchbook, just because she might have use for a new career in driving semi-tractor trailers, but then threw it away. You never knew, in Los Angeles, what was going to crawl out of the woodwork. Tomorrow her ad for a roommate would run. Somebody would come along to save her.

The first person to answer the ad was a green-haired death-punk slam-rock hip-hop biker babe with a chain running from her pierced left ear to her pierced left nostril and a portrait of Charles Manson tattooed on her right biceps. The second was a man of about 30 who, when Alison explained to him she was looking for a female, told her he was going to be female next month unless they rescheduled the operation. The third was a girl from the Valley who said she'd already met Alison in a dream and had given herself permission to feel angry with Alison for invading her space, but her crystals were advising her to give it another chance. Alison shook her head in disbelief, hoping the next respondent would be more suitable, but finally it got to the point that Alison stopped answering the door. Late in the afternoon, somebody knocked so insistently she had to answer it, flinging the door open angrily and saying, "What?"

Michael Mancini stood there, a slip of paper in

his hand, which he handed to her. It was a note from the landlord, informing her that unless he received the rent immediately, he'd have to evict her. Michael shook his head apologetically.

"I'm sorry, Alison," he said. "He dropped this off for me to give to you. Is there anything you can do?" Alison was in too much shock to reply. "Write a bad check if you have to. By the time it bounces, you'll have found somebody." She appreciated what he was trying to do for her, but she wanted to cry anyway.

"That's against the law," she said.

"We're not talking grand larceny," he said. "Just a little floater. Jane and I don't want to see you move. How about your parents?"

She remembered the "swimming lesson" her father had given her when she was little, taking her out into a cold Wisconsin lake until she was over her head, then letting go of her and backing away, forcing her to come after him or drown trying. To some people "sink or swim" was just a saying, but her parents took the philosophy literally. They considered her moving to L.A. along the same lines. It cheered her only a little to note she'd been the captain of the swim team in college.

"I'll find somebody by tomorrow," she told Michael. "I've got a whole bunch of possibilities."

Alison was sitting on a stool at Shooters that night when Sandy found her. For all her overt bitchiness, Sandy was a decent person, even if she didn't want anybody to know. Alison's belief was confirmed when Sandy brought her a drink "on the house," knowing, probably, that Alison was in no position to pay for one.

Sandy smiled. "On a manhunt?" she said. "I don't usually see you in here all by your own self."

"No," Alison said, though that was not strictly accurate. "I mean, yes. Sort of."

"Well then," Sandy said conspiratorially, "I would suggest tighter jeans, more makeup and a lot more attitude." Alison tried to protest but Sandy continued. "Every man in this dive wants to sleep with me, but beauty's only half of it. You gotta learn to play a role, and then—"

"Sandy," Alison interrupted, "I'm looking for one particular guy. His name is Billy . . . something. He shoots pool here." Then she spotted him, leaning on a cue by the third table. "There he is."

Sandy leaned against the bar and studied Billy.

"He's real cute," she said. "So what's going on between you two?"

"Nothing," Alison said. "I just want him to move in with me."

Sandy nodded. "You better learn his last name first," she advised.

As she approached the pool table, Alison watched Billy scratch on the eight ball, cursing. He was putting his cue back in the rack when he saw Alison.

"Ah, well," he said, "I knew there had to be a reason why I scratched. You're bad luck."

"No, I'm not," Alison said, following him to his

table.

"If you're trying to get a line on your old roommate, I haven't seen her since the night I met her here."

"I'm looking for you," Alison said, holding her breath slightly before exhaling, about to take a risk she wished she didn't have to. But then, hadn't her first instinct been that he was earnest and sincere? Maybe she could trust him. "Let's give it a shot. What the hell. If it doesn't work out, you'll move, right?"

He looked at her.

"Too late," he said. "I already found a place."

She was crestfallen. She closed her eyes in frustration. "You did?"

"No," he said. "I was just testing to see if you really wanted me." She didn't like playing games, and had turned to leave when he grabbed her arm to stop her. She looked at him.

"I can move in tomorrow," he said. She nodded in resignation. She had no choice. No choice at all.

"Can I bring anything? Champagne to toast our new relationship?"

"No, Billy," she said. "Just bring a check."

2

EVERYONE WHO LIVED IN MELROSE PLACE had a different reason. For some it was a place to become part of a community, a place to meet people. For others it was a place to hide, a place to build a personal fortress of solitude. Some came expecting to stay only a little while, and ended up staying for years. Others expected to stay for years and never so much as unpacked. For Jane and Michael, it was the place where they had chosen to start their marriage, a chance to live rent free in return for being the super, and put some money in the bank until Michael finished his internship and they could afford a house. This morning it was a place for Michael to sleep, while Jane lay beside him wide awake, watching him. She'd worn a sexy new teddy to bed, but Michael had been so tired when he got home he hadn't even noticed. She decided to give him a second chance.

"Michael," she whispered in his ear. "Michael." He stirred and gave a low grunt. She kissed him on the neck. "I have to be at work in an hour."

"Mmmm hmmm," he replied.

"What time will you be home tonight?"

"Late," he said. "I got the night shift." It was nothing Jane hadn't come to expect other doctors' wives had warned her but just because something was expected didn't mean one couldn't resist it.

"I know they're killing you and the hours are crazy," she said softly, kissing him again on the neck, "and I know it's going to be this way for a while." She nuzzled him behind the ear. "But can you save a little energy tonight for us?"

He rolled over onto his back and faced her, opening one eye, then the other. He reached up and ran his fingers through her short, blond hair.

"Are you insinuating I'm not fulfilling my husbandly duties?" he asked.

"Michael," she said, trying not to sound too serious, "don't you get horny anymore?"

He looked at her, then pulled her toward him and kissed her on the mouth, in the way that had always instantly aroused her, a kiss that meant business. She climbed on top of him and kissed him back, loving the way it felt when his chest filled with air, lifting her up toward the sky. His hands found the spaghetti straps of her teddy, when she began to hear bells ringing. A door bell, to be exact.

"Ignore it," Michael said.

The bell rang again.

"Maybe it's important," she whispered, still kissing him. Michael gave out a groan of animal frustration and rolled Jane off of him.

When he answered the bell Alison stood in the doorway, holding two checks in front of her smiling face.

"Ta da!" she said. "I've got the rent."

"Congratulations," Michael said, taking the checks from her.

"Mine and his," she explained pointing over her shoulder. The name on one of the checks was Billy Campbell. Billy was carrying his only major possession, a Barca-Lounger reclining easy chair, a moving out gift from his father, he'd explained. Alison called him over and introduced him to Michael. The two men shook hands politely.

"Good timing," Michael said, waving the checks in the air. "The owner wanted me to change the locks if I didn't get this by Monday."

"Are you serious?" Alison asked.

"If you haven't figured it out by now, his sole raison d'être is to torment all who cross his path," Michael said, turning to Billy. "Anyway, welcome. It's a good building. The natives are a little weird, but friendly."

"Good," Billy said. "I'm weird but friendly, too."

"I only make a few simple requests," Michael

told him. "One, you pay your rent on time. Two, never knock on this door before eight a.m. unless it's an emergency. And three, don't pee in the pool."

"Too late. Just kidding. Now if you'll excuse me," Billy said, pointing at the Barca-Lounger, which he'd set down beside the pool, "I have to go work on my hernia." When he was gone, Michael asked Alison if Billy was her boyfriend. She stared at him as if he had a duck growing out of his forehead.

Upstairs, Rhonda was waking Sandy up to tell her the news. There was a new man in the building, a handsome one at that, and nothing was better news to Rhonda than a handsome man moving into the building.

"Wake up Sandy—Alison's got a new roommate," Rhonda said excitedly, "and he's got it goin' on."

"I know," Sandy said, lying in bed with a blindfold over her eyes. Sandy slept with the same level of intensity and commitment as Rhonda taught aerobics. Nobody at Melrose Place thought it was fair that Sandy looked as beautiful as she did without lifting a finger to achieve it.

"What do you know?" Rhonda asked. "You don't know nothin'. You spend so much time in here sleeping the day away, you could be Dracula's wife."

Sandy pulled the eyeshades down and looked at Rhonda. "His name is Billy Campbell. He's about six feet, brown hair, nice eyes and he can't shoot pool to save his mother's life."

"How did you know all that?" Rhonda wondered.

"Because darlin'," Sandy drawled, "like I've told you—daytime is just rehearsal. Anything, and I mean *anything*, worth knowing happens at night."

In Apartment Three, Billy set his Barca-Lounger down and sat in it, exhausted. He took his sweaty shirt off, sniffed it and then chucked it across the room, trying to cool off, just as Alison walked in, surprised at the sight of bare flesh.

"Excuse me," Alison said. She seemed embarrassed.

"Don't sweat it," Billy said, regretting his word choice.

"I guess I'm just a little nervous. I've never lived with a strange guy before."

"I've never lived with a strange girl before. Have you told your parents?"

"Not yet."

"They'll love me, I guarantee it."

"Maybe we should talk about privacy," Alison told him. This conversation would be so much easier with another female, she thought. She wouldn't be so worried, for one thing, about coming off as territorial.

"What do you mean?" Billy said.

"Your room, my room. Neither of us entering the other's room without knocking first."

"Goes without saying," he said. "What happens when I bring home a babe and we're going at it on the couch?"

"Going at it?" she said.

"My social life."

Alison felt her heart sink, even though he'd told her that was why he wanted to move out, the first time he'd babbled to her. "Wait a minute," she said. "You're not going to be bringing girls back to this apartment, are you?"

"Hopefully, yes," Billy said, looking incredulous.

"And where am I supposed to be?"

"I don't know. How about in your bedroom, reading a book?"

"While you and some bimbo are doing . . . things . . . on my living room sofa? I don't think so."

"Suddenly she's a bimbo?" Billy said.

"All right, all right," Alison said, putting up her hands, knowing she had to agree. "But no more than one night a week. That goes for both of us. Now, come into the kitchen. I want to show you something." She opened the refrigerator door. She'd put notes with her name on them on all the food items that were hers, after Natalie had eaten half a chocolate mousse pie Alison had been saving, claiming it was an "accident." "The top two shelves are mine," she told Billy, "the bottom two are yours. That way there's never any confusion." Billy pulled out a jar of peanut butter and examined it.

"You put your name on everything?"

"Just a precaution."

"What if I'm dying for some peanut butter and I'm all out? I find it really hard to control myself around food."

"There's a twenty-four hour convenience store down the block. Now, as for the utilities . . ."

"Wait a minute. You mean I can't eat your peanut butter, even if I've got a mad, insatiable craving?"

"I'd prefer you didn't," Alison said, proud of herself for taking a stand.

"Let me ask you something, Alison. Do you take baths?"

"Of course I take baths," she said.

"Well I don't. I take showers. Baths waste water, not to mention the gas it takes to heat the water."

"So what are you saying?"

"You pay for your food, I pay for my food. You pay for your hot water, I pay for my hot water." Alison saw the logic. They could agree to general principles, she knew, but being a stickler for absolute details was absurd.

"Okay," she gave in. "You can eat my peanut butter."

"Just a spoonful here and there, in case of emergencies. And you can have mine when you run out."

"Before I forget, one more thing." She led him to the bathroom, where she pointed to the toilet. "Above and beyond everything else I've told you, you must always, always, leave the seat down. Say it back to me. The seat is left down."

"The seat is left down," Billy said. "No problem."

When Alison returned to the bathroom five minutes later, the seat was up.

*   *   *

Rhonda was headed for class when she saw Matt swimming laps, such as they were, for the pool was not exactly Olympic size. She told him the news of the new boy in town, knowing he'd be interested. He said he'd worked a lot of overtime recently and hadn't seen Alison's new roommate.

"I know," Rhonda said. "I haven't seen you all week. I thought maybe we could catch a movie this Saturday."

"I'd like to, but I'm leading a program over at the center. 'How to enjoy a drug-free Saturday night.'"

"I'm leading my own program, 'How to enjoy a date-free Saturday night.' Where are you going?"

"Bowling," Matt said.

"Bowling?" Rhonda said, making a face.

"Yeah," Matt said. "Believe it or not, most of these kids have never picked up a bowling ball in their lives. Join us. You and me and fifteen street kids. We could get married and adopt them all, like that Lucille Ball movie . . ."

"*Yours, Mine and Ours,*" Rhonda said. She liked the idea of being married, though Matt was, as some might say, "a confirmed bachelor." Why was it that gay men were so much easier to get along with?

Just then, Billy walked past, carrying another load from his car.

"He's cute," Matt said.

"Hands off," Rhonda said. "I saw him first."

In point of fact, Alison had seen him first, second and third, and still wasn't quite sure what to make of Billy Campbell. She was in the kitchen, sorting through her boxes of Hamburger Helper, and thinking about which to make for dinner when she heard samba music of all things, emanating from Billy's bedroom. The door was partially open. Billy was dancing, all by himself, carefully following a set of footprints he'd placed on the floor. When she knocked he looked as if he'd been caught stealing cookies from the cookie jar.

"How's the unpacking?" she asked.

He turned the music off. "Fine. I basically think I got everything in."

"What exactly do you *do*, anyway?"

"I'm a writer."

"A writer? What kind of writer?"

"A novelist," he said, sounding as if he wasn't quite comfortable making the claim.

"You mean, like Jackie Collins?"

"No, I mean like Norman Mailer," he said, sounding hurt. "You don't know who he is, do you?"

"Of course I know who he is," she replied. "I was summa cum laude at the University of Wisconsin, with an English major. Have you sold anything?"

"What is it you do?" he asked, probably to change the subject, Alison thought. He hadn't sold anything. Maybe he was one of those people who claim to be "writers" just because they want so badly to be writers, but don't actually write anything.

"I work at D and D Advertising," she told him, trying to sound proud of herself. "I assist executives and serve as a conduit of information."

"You answer the phones," he said, seeing right through her.

"Basically," she said. "It's an entry-level position. I was hired because of my communication skills."

"And because male ad men like the idea of having a cute girl taking their messages. Don't you think?"

"I'm not cute," she protested. "Okay, I mean, I am cute, but telling me they hired me for my looks is a lousy patronizing thing to say, though it doesn't surprise me, coming from 'the next Norman Mailer,' who, incidentally, hates women."

"Just asking," he said, as Alison stormed out.

Downstairs, Jake Hanson sat in his apartment, listening to a busy signal. He'd just finished working on a house in Burbank, and was trying to get hold of a contractor he knew in Santa Monica who, Jake had heard, needed someone to frame a deck. Jake was a carpenter by trade, and times were lean. At the beginning of the recession, when new construction fell off, those people who couldn't afford to move or build had put additions on their homes, and there was work. Now, deeper into the recession, Jake felt he was lucky if somebody needed him to hang a kitchen cabinet or screw down a countertop. He'd re-dialed the contractor when he heard a knock at the door.

It was Kelly.

They stared at each other a moment. Jake wasn't sure what to say, but Kelly seemed angry.

"Hi," he said.

"Why didn't you return any of my calls?" she asked him. "I left a bunch of messages on your machine. Didn't you get them?"

"Kelly," he said, "yeah, I got them. I've been busy. We were putting in a nursery in a house in Burbank . . ."

"Jake, if you don't want to see me then I guess I have to deal with that, but I think you owe me some kind of explanation." Her lower lip trembled slightly, as if she was about to cry.

He hated seeing her so upset, knowing it was his fault, though he wasn't quite sure how they'd become so involved. He'd met Kelly when her mother hired him to work on their house, to get it ready for her wedding. Playfully, they'd explored a mutual infatuation because there was no denying that Kelly was adorable and feisty, and there was something fresh about her, like a crisp, cold apple. Furthermore, it was flattering, the way her eyes lit up when she saw him. It restored his ego, and lately his ego had been in need of restoring. When she'd invited him to be her date at the wedding, her mother's second, he'd at first declined but then he'd shown up, not wanting to hurt the kid's feelings. Then she'd wanted to kiss him, and he'd wanted to kiss her . . . Maybe that had been a mistake. Now feelings were involved. He was more sure of Kelly's feelings than of his own, but he knew that in both instances, they ran deep.

"I mean," she continued, "you show up at my mom's wedding and say we should try to make it work, and the next thing I know, you've disappeared."

"It was just a date," Jake said. "I don't remember planning our future together."

"Don't tell me you didn't feel anything."

"And what if I did?" he said. "What do you want me to do, hang out at the Beverly Hills Beach Club all summer?" That was the problem. In theory, a relationship with Kelly looked good, even promising. In the real world, it looked impossible. There were too many differenes.

"I don't know," she said. He could see her tears welling up. "I just wish you'd stop avoiding me because it's making me crazy." She turned to leave.

He grabbed her by the arm to stop her.

She jerked her arm away, though he was only trying to calm her down. "Don't touch me," she shouted. "I was worried about you! I thought something had happened. How was I supposed to know? How could you do this to me? You know how I feel about you."

It was a valid question, Jake knew. How could people make each other feel so good and so bad, sometimes simultaneously? What were you supposed to do when you wanted something bad but knew it was wrong? Do you go ahead and take it, or do you turn it away? Either way it made you seem a selfish jerk—you couldn't win.

"I'm sorry," he told her. "I guess I don't know how to deal with it."

"If you think I'm just some stupid lovesick teenager making a fool of myself, just tell me and

I'll leave," she said. "But if you really feel something for me, but you're afraid of it because you think you're too old, or I'm too young, well . . . I don't care. I don't care what people think and I don't know why you care either."

Jake wanted to take her in his arms. Instead he pushed her away. "I don't care," he said. "I'm just trying to do what's right."

"What's right is what you feel," she said. "Anything else and you're just lying to yourself."

"Sometimes you gotta lie to yourself," he said, "to keep life running smoothly." It was a fact of life he doubted a girl her age understood yet.

"I see," she said. "Well, I guess I'll just go home then."

"Kelly!" he said, weakening.

"What is it?"

"I hate moral dilemmas," he told her. It was not, as Sandy had suggested, a case of him not using his head. His head was saying a million things, his heart, only one.

"What's the problem?" she asked. "Don't you think I'm pretty?"

"The problem is," he said, "I think you're beautiful. How about dinner tomorrow night?"

"Do you mean that?" she asked. "Or am I going to walk out of here and never hear from you again?"

"I don't think either one of us is going to get off that easy," he said. Maybe by tomorrow night he'd think of something. In the meantime, all he wanted to do, more than anything else in the world, was kiss her. So he did.

3

RHONDA BLAIR KNEW SHE WAS SECRETLY jealous of Alison, who complained of hair in the sink and jockstraps on the towel rack, but even so, had constant, albeit platonic, male companionship. At 30, Rhonda was one of the oldest tenants at Melrose Place. 30 was still too young to consider herself an old maid, she knew. All the same, she'd begun to notice that the lonely nights seemed lonelier, the hard days harder, the older she got. Some days, it was hard not to take it out on the students in her aerobics classes, because Rhonda had found that a good vigorous workout could usually cure whatever funk she was in.

She worked out of a gym just off San Vincente,

and today she had her eye on an attractive black man in the back row who she'd never seen before. He appeared to be on the point of total exhaustion, but still having a good time. Rhonda felt a delightful sense of power when she had men in such a position, and wandered over to him while staying in step, calling out the changes and cadence.

"You getting any of this?" she asked him as she continued moving.

"Mmmghtrahhnngh," he said, which she translated as "I'm trying."

She kept her eye on him as she allowed the class to cool down and stretch. He seemed to be keeping his eye on her. When the music stopped, and the rest of the class toweled off and departed, he lingered a bit, maybe just to catch his breath, but maybe he had something more on his mind. It was worth finding out.

"I haven't seen you before," Rhonda said, strolling over to him.

"I'm Daniel," he told her. "Nice class." She threw him her towel. He dried himself, but when she gestured for him to throw it back, he held onto it. "No way. I want to take it home and never wash it."

She put her hands on her hips, impatient. "Please," he said. "I'll trade you—let me keep it and I'll take you out to dinner." He didn't waste much time.

"I don't even know you," she said. "How do I know you don't have a house just full of smelly old towels?"

"So get to know me," he said. She considered.

Her first impulse was, she liked him. She decided to trust it.

"Okay," she said. "Sure, why not. How'd you hear about my class, anyway?"

"Every cute girl I've ever met in this town tells me she owes her body to you, so I figured I'd go straight to the source," he said.

Was that all this was, a cheap come-on? She told him she wasn't so sure anymore. Maybe a date was a bad idea.

"I'm kidding, I'm kidding," he said. "How about Friday at eight? Café Luna?"

She reconsidered. It could be worth the risk. "I'll meet you there," she said. If things went well, he could pick her up in his limo for the second date.

At D&D Advertising, Alison was too busy putting through calls to even think about a social life. She had none and, for the time being anyway, she didn't mind at all. She was trying to locate an executive for a client when Hal Barber suddenly appeared, and sat on the edge of her desk. She put the client on hold. Hal asked if she could help him out, offering a questionnaire for her to fill out. He explained that they were developing a new Canyon Country Cooler ad campaign, aimed at people in their early twenties. He promised not to sue for the damages she'd done to his car if she helped him out by answering a few questions. A sense of relief swept over her.

"I'm not going to get graded on this, am I?" she asked.

"Maybe on penmanship," he said with a playful wink. "Just be honest."

After her class, Rhonda had practically flown down to Couture, the boutique on Melrose where Jane worked. It was a *très* trendy shop with party dresses and club clothes, most of which Rhonda couldn't afford in a million years, which was why she told Jane she needed her help. "What's wrong?" Jane asked.

"This guy asked me out on a date," Rhonda said.

"That's wonderful," Jane said.

"It's fabulous," Rhonda corrected her, "except I have nothing in my closet. Can you find me something I can wear tonight and then return tomorrow for a full refund?"

"I didn't hear that," Jane said, smiling.

While they sorted through the racks, Rhonda was a bundle of nerves, trying to think of what impression she wanted to make. "It must be great to be married and not have to worry about dating anymore," she said.

"It's wonderful," Jane admitted. "When I get to see Michael. Except when I'm at home, he's working, and when he's at home, I'm here."

"You're unbelievable," Rhonda said. "You're Superwoman."

"No," Jane said. She looked Rhonda in the eye. "I just made some choices."

"You're still lucky," Rhonda said, flipping

through a set of sequined mini skirts. "You found
Mr. Right. I keep finding Mr. Well . . . Mr. I-Don't-
Think-So. Mr. Who's-Kidding-Who-Here? I keep
looking for the right person but I never know."

"You'll know," Jane said her voice firm. "Here
we go." She held up a simple little black number with
a plunging neckline, the kind of thing only an aerobics instructor could look good in. While Jane rang
up the "sale," Rhonda remembered a line from the
Shakespeare class she'd taken in college, "the course
of true love never did run straight," or something like
that. Never did, Rhonda thought, never would.

Rhonda was trying on the dress that night
when she heard across the courtyard the sounds of
tango music coming from Billy and Alison's apartment. She wondered, momentarily, if the two of
them were dancing.

Coming home from work, Alison paused by the
pool and heard the music as well. When she opened
the apartment door, she caught Billy dancing cheek
to cheek with a broom. It was a nice-looking
broom, but nothing she'd ever felt like dancing
with. Billy froze in his tracks when he saw her, a
hot Gato Barbieri number blasting from the stereo.

"What are you doing?" Alison asked.

"Me?" he said. "Uh . . . practicing."

"Practicing?" she repeated.

"My dance steps," he said, turning off the
music. "This is a little embarrassing."

Alison waited.

"I don't exactly support myself . . . writing."

She waited some more.

"So in order to move out of my parents' place, I had to find a job that would leave my days free to write, which is really hard, okay?"

"Billy, what is it you do for a living?" She was afraid to hear the answer. What if he was a gigolo who seduced wealthy Argentinean widows?

"I teach dance at Arthur Murray."

She tried to keep a straight face but couldn't, and burst out laughing.

"You can laugh if you want," he said.

"I will," she said, calming down. "It's just—it's hard to picture, that's all. I didn't mean to laugh at you."

"I was desperate," he said. "You take what you can get. I went in and then I lied about my experience, which is basically senior prom and a bunch of Fred and Ginger movies, so I bought a book and these tapes. Right now I'm about one lesson ahead of the class."

"Don't let me interrupt," she said, heading for the bathroom and a long soak. After the day she'd had, though, the good laugh had gone a long way toward restoring her spirits.

"Actually," Billy called after her, "I was wondering if you'd practice with me."

"I'd love to practice with you, Billy," she said, pausing by the bathroom door. "All my life I've wanted to learn how to tango. Not."

* * *

At Shooters, the joint was jumping. Outside, a good dozen chopped-out Harleys sat at the curb, snarling with chrome and black leather, glistening in the neon. Inside were the usual suspects, college boys with their caps on backward, heavy metal rockers with their heads on backward, daddies' girls and ladies' men and even a few ladies' girls and daddies' men, rich men and poor men, beggars and thieves, doctors, lawyers and, seated at the bar, a guy wearing a Cleveland Indians cap, and next to him, a character dressed like Ingrid Bergman, saying she needed to speak to Rick about the letters of transit. From the waitress station, Sandy watched as Jake entered with a blond girl on his arm.

It was Kelly, and tonight she looked very impressed.

Jake wondered if she'd ever been in a bar before. "Bad influence" should be his middle name, he thought. "Welcome to my home away from home," he told her. "Good food, good music . . ." He saw Sandy approaching, with a look on her face that told him she meant to cause trouble. "Lousy service. Hello Sandy."

"Hello darlin'," Sandy cooed, looking down her nose at Kelly. "What'll it be? Beer and a chocolate milk?"

"Two chocolate milks," Jake said with a smirk. Sandy never approved of any of the women he talked to at Shooters, and he didn't expect her to change with Kelly.

"We don't have chocolate milk—that was a joke, stupid," she said.

"I'll have a Coke," Kelly said quietly.

"And I'll have a beer," Jake said.

"Fine," Sandy said disdainfully. "It's your life."

"What's her problem?" Kelly asked, once Sandy was gone. She suspected it was the same problem her friend Donna had. *She'd* spent the whole afternoon telling Kelly how Jake wasn't right for her, how he was too old and too experienced, as if there were some law carved in granite somewhere that said everything had to be equal before you were allowed to fall in love.

"Got a couple weeks?" Jake said.

"Actually I really don't care."

"Good answer," he told her.

"Oh God, no," Kelly said. "I don't believe it." She was staring at the door. Jake turned and looked. He saw Kelly's friends Donna and Steve, and her step brother David. He recognized them from the wedding. Obviously, they were there to check up on Kelly and protect her from the big bad Jake.

He asked Kelly. "What are your friends doing here?"

"I told Donna where I was going so she could cover for me in case my mom called her house," Kelly said, her cheeks flushed with embarrassment.

"You're keeping this from your mom?" Jake said.

"I have to," Kelly said. "She'd kill me if she knew."

This is what I get, Jake thought, for dating a 17 year-old. He remembered when he was 17, and even then he hadn't dated 17-year-olds. In fact, he'd had a relationship with a 26-year-old divorcée, which, in part, was why he had some sympathy with what Kelly might be feeling. Somehow, though, it wasn't the same for girls, or maybe just being on the other end of the equation, Jake felt differently about it.

Her friends joined them. Kelly immediately pulled Donna off to have a word with her, just as Sandy brought the drinks, a big smirk on her face.

"Well hey, this is turning into a regular sweet sixteen party, huh Jake?" she said. "What can I get you all to drink?"

"Whatever's on tap," Steve said, trying to sound older. David nodded in complete agreement.

"I'll need to see some I.D.," Sandy told them.

"We're with Jake," Steve said. "He'll vouch for us."

Over by the pool tables, Kelly was furiously asking Donna what she thought she was doing.

"We were worried about you," Donna said.

"Why?"

"Kelly, he's too old, you have nothing in common—you're obsessed!"

"I am not obsessed," Kelly said. "What we have between us is something you don't understand, and it's none of your business."

"It becomes my business when I have to lie to your mom about where you go at night."

"Then don't," Kelly said.

Back at the table, Jake listened patiently as Steve and David tried to scare him off, trying to make it sound like a friendly warning.

"One thing you should know about dating

Kelly is that her friends are never far behind," Steve said.

"And there's lots more where we come from," David added. Jake smiled.

"I see what you're trying to do," he said. "Shouldn't you let Kelly make her own decisions? How would you like it?" Before they could answer, Sandy returned with the drinks.

"Jake, I just decided," she told them, setting the sodas down. "If you're going to date high school girls, I'm going to date high school boys." She sat on Steve's lap and put her arm around him, her mini skirt riding high up her thigh. "Starting with this one. You're cute."

"Steve Sanders," he said. "Nice to meet you. By the way Jake, I think this is fair. I withdraw all objections." There was something about the way Sandy could wrap virtually any man she wanted around her little finger that Jake admired very much. And feared.

"Where y'all from?" Sandy asked.

"Beverly Hills," Steve said.

"Ooh, handsome and rich," she drawled. "And so Kelly's from Beverly Hills too." She looked at Jake. "Now I'm beginnin' to understand."

"Sandy's an actress," Jake explained to the others. "Everything she says is a line. One way or the other."

"Shut up, Jake," Sandy snapped.

"My mom's an actress," Steve said. "Samantha Sanders. She's on the TV show "The Hartley House." Jake smiled again as he watched Sandy's

face light up, realizing she was sitting on the lap of
a person she could actually use.

"I love her," Sandy said. "I would do anything
to meet her."

"Let me give you my number," Steve said.
"You could come by."

Kelly returned to the table, where she picked up
her purse and asked Jake if they could leave. Jake
had the sense she and Donna had not quite finished
their dispute.

"Nice to see you all. I appreciate your concern," Kelly told her friends sarcastically.

Outside they went for a stroll, past a shop that
sold Mexican Day-of-the-Dead masks, past another
that sold nothing but circa 1950 Coke machines
and paraphernalia, and past a shop displaying large
fiber glass horses and cows in the window. On the
street people of all ages and walks of life cruised
past, tourists, boys from East L.A. in low-riders,
balding playboys in Mercedes convertibles with
gold chains around their necks. Jake followed
behind Kelly until she calmed down. She finally
stopped and turned to him.

"Jake, I'm sorry about that—I had no idea they
were going to be there."

"Kelly," Jake said. "Maybe you should go
home with your friends."

"What do you mean?"

"Because they're right. Because you belong with
them, not me. Because I don't want to complicate
your life."

"But what about the other day?" Kelly said.

"All the things we talked about. You said you thought I was beautiful . . ."

"C'mon Kelly," Jake said. He'd hoped, some time during the night, that maybe, without having to force the issue, they might simply agree that they'd gone as far as they could go. In part, he was hoping she'd reach that conclusion on her own, and then persuade him, because he didn't know for certain what to do. "I work construction, Kelly. I've got lots of age and all kinds of experience on you. My problems, you don't even know about."

So much she didn't know. Jake thought, briefly, of his old man, moving from cocktail party to cocktail party, mistress to mistress, a real good-time Charlie, he was, before leaving Jake and his mother all alone. 'Admit it, you're a chip off the old block, just like me, love 'em and leave 'em,' his father had said once, when he'd had too many martinis.

"Maybe your friends are smarter than we are," Jake said.

"Maybe they're not," Kelly said. "Except for my friend Dylan. He was right about one thing. He said you had a great heart but you didn't know how to open it. Maybe I'm just a kid, but I thought for a while I could have helped you with that."

She ran back to the bar, where her friends were getting into their car, and left with them. As she drove away, Jake wondered why it had to be so hard. He only knew he longed for things to be less complicated. Maybe he was dreaming.

4

ON THURSDAY NIGHT, JANE SPENT THE
afternoon buying shrimp and scallions and Japanese
sticky rice, preparing a meal for Michael, who was
going to be home early for a change. Four brand
new black candles sat on the table, in brass candle
holders. As she cooked, she sipped a glass of red
wine, while vintage Aretha Franklin played from
the stereo. When she heard Michael's car pull up,
she changed the music to soft jazz, lit the candles
and poured a second glass of wine. Michael stag-
gered in the door, looking like he'd just driven five
hundred miles of bumpy gravel road in a Yugo.

"Oh God, I'm beat," he said with his eyes
closed, dropping his jacket on the floor where he

stood. Total system failure seemed imminent. Jane handed him the glass of wine and kissed him. "Thank you. Thank you. Thank you," he said. "You smell great." He opened his eyes, noting the romantically set table with surprise. "What's all this?"

"It's called dinner," Jane said. "It's the time when most married couples sit down and relax over a nice meal and talk to each other."

"What's the occasion?" he asked, knowing immediately it was a bonehead question. There shouldn't have to be an occasion.

"Something in the back of my mind told me if we didn't spend some quality time together soon, we'd be headed for trouble," she said, trying to get her point across without coming down too hard on him. He looked worried.

"Are we in trouble?"

"I don't know," she said. "What do you think?"

He set his wine glass down and approached her, throwing his arms around her. "I sure hope not," he said softly, barely above a whisper. "Because, when the day starts stretching into eighteen hours, and I've had the crap knocked out of me by every ego-maniacal physician on the staff and I've seen so many bodies turned inside out that—"

Jane put her finger to his mouth to shush him.

"Anyway," he finished, "the point is, when things get rough, I think of you. You're what keeps me going. If I didn't have you to think about, I don't know if I'd make it."

She stood on her toes and kissed him. That was what marriage was for, after all, a respite, two people providing each other with shelter from the storms of life. Sometimes thinking of Michael was what kept her going at the boutique when things got crazy. She was undoing his tie when the phone rang.

"Dammit!" she said, breaking off the kiss.

"Ignore it," Michael said.

"I can't," she said. "Nobody calls at eleven unless it's important." It was the landlord.

Something about a bounced check.

Alison was almost asleep when she heard the pounding on the door. Billy met her going to answer it, wearing only his boxer shorts. When Michael told her Billy's check had bounced, she was furious. Michael said the landlord was furious as well, and that Billy had to come up with a cashier's check tomorrow. She waited to confront him until after Michael had left.

"They don't pay me at Arthur Murray until next week," Billy offered as his excuse. "I thought I could cover the check before the landlord cashed it."

"I guess you thought wrong, didn't you?" Alison said. She'd believed she'd narrowly averted getting evicted, and now this.

"It's just a temporary financial setback," Billy said. "Have a little faith."

"Billy, this may come as a shock to you, but

I'm not living with you on the basis of your stunning good looks or your sparkling personality. I'm living with you because you promised to come up with your share of the rent, promptly and in full."

"Alison, I'll get you the money. It's not a big deal."

"Maybe not to you," she said. "You can always crawl back to Mommy and Daddy and your cozy little bungalow in the Valley, but when I moved out of my house to go to college it was for good. Excuse me for taking life a little seriously, but if I don't pay the rent, I'm out on the street."

"They wouldn't . . ."

"They would. They'd have to. And they'd be right. That's how it works, Billy. Either come up with the rent or I start looking for a new roommate."

Billy was gone by the time she woke up. She'd felt bad about being so hard on him, but she hadn't said anything she hadn't meant. On her way to her car, she saw Jane swimming laps in the pool. Jane said Billy had knocked on their door at seven in the morning, promising a cashier's check by the end of the day. Jane apologized if Michael seemed a little grumpy, but the affair about the bounced check had interrupted a more important affair involving good wine and a romantic candlelight dinner.

Alison apologized, but still felt responsible.

Traffic was bad, surprise surprise, though there were no shootings or Terminator cyborgs from the future strewing wreckage in their wake, so she supposed things could have been worse. At work, she ran into Hal Barber in the parking lot. He greeted her with a broad smile on his face and told her that he'd appreciated her help with the questionnaire.

"'Canyon Country Coolers: The Passion Starts Here,'" he called out to her. "What do you think?" She walked into the building with him.

"I love it," she said.

"Does it say 'twenties?'"

"Definitely."

"I like that word, 'passion,'" he said, using a hand gesture to spell it out in the air. "It implies commitment, but it also says sex."

"All in one word," Alison said. "That's really great. That's what I want to be able to do, someday."

"You will," he said. "Listen, the client's having a little party tonight to unveil the new flavor. If you're free, you could join me. Be a good opportunity for you to meet some people."

"Really?" she said.

"Really."

She told him she'd love to, though she'd have to run home and change first. He said he'd pick her up. Going to parties like that was exactly what she'd hoped would happen to her. That was where the real deals got made, or at least where the promotions originated. It was funny how good luck and bad luck often happened at the same time.

She was waiting at the curb outside Melrose Place for Hal to pick her up that night. He had said, "I'll be in the black BMW with the dented door." As she paced the sidewalk Rhonda appeared, looking fabulous in her little black dress, accessorized with funky heels and killer patterned tights. Alison was wearing a dress she would have considered more casual elegant than sexy—a dark silk print with a Buster Brown collar—though Rhonda told her she looked hot.

"Thanks," Alison said. "That's what Billy thought. I have to tell you, it was weird, getting dressed for a party with him there. I mean, I liked the compliment, but it was just strange."

"You'll get used to it, girlfriend," Rhonda said. "I've got a hot date tonight with a man I met in class and I'm hoping for a compliment or two myself."

"Don't do anything I wouldn't do," Alison said.

"That's exactly what Matt told me," Rhonda said with a wink, getting into her car. "See you later."

The Canyon Cooler reception was being held at the top of the Bel Age Hotel, around a large rooftop swimming pool surrounded by plants and sculpture with delicate backlighting, and a panoramic view of Los Angeles below; the city lights twinkling on the desert floor like the scattered embers of a fire. It still amazed Alison, how beautiful L.A. could seem sometimes, though usually it was at night, and you had to squint. Standing poolside were an assortment of beautiful people, men in tuxedos and ponytails, smashing women in gowns that cost as much as Alison paid in rent for an entire year, if not more, and they probably only wore them once. Sometimes L.A. still made her feel like a midwestern farmer's daughter. Tonight, she decided, it was time to fit in.

"Canyon Cooler?" a waiter asked.

"Do we really have a choice?" Hal said, taking two drinks and handing one to Alison.

She took a sip. It tasted like a cross between baby-food and Listerine. Hal told her it was mango, the new flavor.

"Pretend you love it," he mouthed. "Come on, let me introduce you to some people."

They circled the pool. Alison thought she saw Mary Tyler Moore ducking into the bathroom; she wondered how long she'd have to live in L.A. before the glimpse of a possible celebrity became blasé to her. She'd once nearly had a heart attack when she saw Tom Cruise on his motorcycle at a stop light. Another time, she could have sworn she'd been stuck behind Grampa from the original Munsters in a line at the bank.

"Tom Addison," Hal said, touching an older gentleman at the elbow. "This is Alison Parker. Tom is President of Canyon Coolers. Alison works at D and D."

"Very nice to meet you," Alison said.

"Pleased to meet you as well," Addison replied.

"'The passion starts here,'" Alison said cheerfully, raising her glass to him.

He looked confused. "I beg your pardon?" the President of Canyon Coolers said.

"Nothing actually—nice seeing you, Tom," Hal said, pulling Alison away.

"What? Did I do something wrong?" she whispered.

"Not exactly," Hal said. "It's just that we haven't made the presentation yet, so Tom hasn't heard the ad line."

"Oh God," Alison said. Her first contact and she'd made a fool of herself. "He must think I was coming on to him."

"Don't worry," Hal said. "When he does hear the line, it'll ring a bell and he'll probably think he thought of it himself. Come on, let's see if we can find us some real drinks, and I'll introduce you to one of the partners. I think he's around . . ."

"Hal?" Alison said. He turned to look at her. "Thanks for bringing me here. This is really amazing. It's everything I dreamed one of these parties would be like."

"It's just a product launch," he said dismissively. "For a wine cooler that tastes like the air freshener in a ten-dollar-a-night motel room."

"I know," she said, pouring her drink into a plant. She took another look around, trying to absorb the glamour of it all anyway. "What can I say? I'm easily impressed."

At the Café Luna, Billy Dee Williams was sitting in a booth by the bar, but Rhonda hardly noticed him, paying complete attention to the handsome man sitting across the table from her. Daniel was wearing an Armani suit that made him look trim and fit, even if her aerobics class earlier in the week had proven otherwise. He had a lovely smile and seemed sincerely interested in her. Rhonda practically had to beg him, for instance, to get him to talk about himself.

"I got my MBA from Pepperdine last year, so now I'm just out here doing the entrepreneur thing, trying to make some bucks," he said, finishing his veal piccata. He had a tendency to talk with his mouth full, but Rhonda was more than willing to overlook the bad habit, because he also had a tendency to pay her lovely compliments, which more than compensated for his lack of table manners.

"Wow," she said. "So you're trying to start your own company?"

"So to speak," he said. "How'd you get into teaching aerobics, anyway?"

"I'm a failed ballet dancer," she said. "I once thought I'd be in a major company by now, but if you don't make it by the time you're twenty-one, forget it."

"Yeah, but you do what you do so well."

"Thanks."

"And you're really great with people. The people in your class really respect and look up to you."

"You think?"

"Definitely. I noticed. They were all wearing the same kind of aerobics shoe as you. I'll bet they all go out and buy the same leotards too."

"Aw, I don't know," Rhonda said, wondering if she were blushing. Where had this man come from?

All his flattery and praise, a girl could only take so much of it, and she intended to let him know, just as soon as he reached the point of saturation.

"That's why you'd be so perfect to sell The Source," he said casually.

"Say what?" she said.

"The Source," he repeated. He pulled a packet of capsules from his jacket pocket and set them on the table in front of Rhonda. "Six tiny capsules, taken three times a day with meals. It's an all-natural, totally potent vitamin/herbal energy storehouse. You'd get thirty percent of every sale."

"You want me to sell vitamins?" she said, still having a hard time believing that this whole date had been nothing more than an elaborate sales pitch.

"They're not just vitamins," he said.

She didn't know whether to throw a drink in his face or cry. Or both. "I can't do that," she told him.

"Gee. I thought you'd jump at the opportunity," he said. "I guess then you won't be wanting any dessert. Oh waiter . . ."

She was glad they'd come in separate cars, because she couldn't bear the thought of riding home with him, and she hated having wasted two hours cleaning her apartment with the expectation of company. One thing was for sure—Daniel wasn't Mr. Right. He wasn't even Mr. Close. She'd laugh, if she wasn't so disappointed.

5

SANDY FOUND JAKE PLAYING PINBALL AT
Shooters, standing at the machine like a rock with
little wasted effort or emotion. She leaned against
the machine, careful not to tilt it, and said hello. He
didn't look up.

"Hi."

"Look, Jake, I just wanted to apologize for the
other night," she said. "I was out of line. Your personal life is none of my business."

"Okay," he said. "Apology accepted."

"I just don't want you to be mad at me. I want
us to be friends. Between this place and home, I see
your face ten times a day. It'd be easier if I knew
you didn't hate me."

"How could I hate you, Sandy," he said, looking up as a ball slid down the drain.

"Oh, lots of people do," she said flippantly. "So, are you seeing her or not? Not that it's any of my business."

"I'll keep you posted," he said, handing her his empty beer bottle.

Around the corner at 4616 Melrose Place, a black BMW with a dent in the door sat at the curb. Hal had offered to walk Alison up to her apartment. She'd told him it wasn't necessary, but it seemed important to him to play the gentleman, so she didn't protest.

"Thanks Hal," she told him when they'd reached her door, putting her key in the lock. "I had a great time. And I really appreciate you introducing me to all those people."

"My pleasure," he said, leaning against the wall. She'd worried that he'd had too much to drink, but she hadn't noticed any swerving or red lights run on their way over. If this were a date, she supposed the man would be waiting for a kiss, but this wasn't a date. It wasn't, was it?

"Well," she said, feeling awkward. "Good night." She opened the door, but as she did, he followed her in.

"Did I ever mention that aside from being smart and ambitious, I also think you're extremely sexy?" he said.

Now she knew he had something in mind. She decided to play it cool.

"Oh, trust me, I'm not."

"How about a little drink before we call it a night?" he said. "Maybe a little tour of your apartment."

"There's not much to see," she said, taking a step backward.

"That's all right," he said, leaning toward her and leering at her. "Everything I need to see is right here." He put his arm around her and was trying to kiss her when she spun away.

As she spun away, she felt him grab at her skirt. "Hal, don't!" she said. Her heart raced but she wasn't frightened. He stopped his pursuit and stood with his hands on his hips, his head tilted to the side.

"Alison, I'm really disappointed," he told her. "You don't want me to be disappointed, do you?" There was more than a bit of a threat in his voice.

"I thought this was just business," she said, looking for anything nearby that she could hit him with, if it came to that.

"Oh, come on Alison. Everything isn't business," he whined. "I introduce you to half the creative exec's, and now you're blowing me off? Where are you from?" He took another step toward her.

"I want you to leave," she said firmly. He took another step, his body language thoroughly menacing.

"Oh come on, Alison—one little drink."

She heard a noise from the hallway. It was Billy.

"What's going on here?" Billy asked, his face grim.

"Who's he?" Hal said, stunned.

"I'm her husband, slimeball," Billy said.

"You never told me you were married," Hal told Alison.

She thought a moment. "You never asked," she said. Billy took another step toward them.

Hal looked at him imploringly. "Your wife has been leading me on," Hal protested, holding up one hand as if he were taking a pledge.

"I heard the whole thing," Billy said. "Now I suggest you get the hell out of here before I throw you through the wall like a cartoon cat."

"Billy, leave him alone," Alison said. "Hal, leave. I'll see you at work."

"Not if I can help it," Hal said, slamming the door behind him.

When he was gone, Alison collapsed on the couch. She might have cried, but she was too angry. Billy sat on the couch next to her and took her hand in his.

"You okay?" he asked.

"Yeah, I'm fine," she said, taking a deep breath. She shook her head in disbelief and sniffed. "For a person who's about to lose her job, I'm just swell."

"He can't fire you for not sleeping with him," Billy said.

"I can't believe I'm so stupid," she said. "I should have seen this coming a mile away. I thought he saw more in me. It's not fair, Billy. God! I'd like to kill him."

"I would have, if you'd given me the chance."

Alison started to chuckle, remembering the look on Billy's face.

"'I'm her husband, slimeball,'" she said, imitating him. "Maybe that's how I'll introduce you next time. 'This is my husband, Slimeball.' It just sounded so ludicrous."

"It was all I could think of," he said, taking offense at her laughter. "Give me a break. Where would you have been if I hadn't walked in?"

"I think I could have handled it," she said.

"Right," he said. "That's not how it looked to me. You owe me one."

As Hal drove off, a red Mercedes convertible filled the space he'd just vacated, and a girl in an artfully tattered blue jean jacket got out of it. She circled the pool until she reached Jake's apartment, knocking loudly, although it was late, because she had to, no matter how afraid she was. A moment later, Jake answered, wearing only his pajama bottoms.

"Kelly," he said. "What are you doing here?"

"Jake, I'm sorry," she said. "This might not be easy for you, but it's not easy for me either. Can I come in?"

He blocked the way. "Kelly, the minute you walk through that door, we both know what's going to happen," he warned her.

"What's so awful about that?"

"Look, give me a little air, okay?" he said gently. "I've got a lot on my mind right now besides you."

"Like what?"

"Like where my next job is coming from, for

starters," he said. "I don't get to hang out at the Beverly Hills Beach Club all summer with my friends. I've got bills to pay, and if I don't find work soon, I'm out on my ass. I've been there. It blows."

"I know," she said.

"No, you don't," he told her. The way she could look at him though, with those huge penetrating, pleading eyes . . . "Look, I'm going to call you, I promise."

"Don't say that if you don't mean it," she said.

"I mean it," he insisted. "I just have to get my life together a little bit."

"Okay," she said, taking a step back.

It broke his heart to see how hard this was on her.

"I understand. I really do."

Before she could leave, he took a step toward her and put his arm around her waist. He held her close and kissed her. She kissed him back, waiting, willing to do anything he told her, trusting him absolutely. She made him feel powerful, and the feeling was intoxicating and heady. She was doing everything right. It made things difficult.

"Sweet Kelly," he said. "What do you even see in me?"

"I must see something," she said, "or I wouldn't be making such a fool out of myself."

"You're not," he told her. "You just picked yourself a challenge, that's all."

As he watched her go, he was filled half with relief, half with regret. There was so much they could do and be together, such a long road he knew they could travel, and he wanted to take the first step. He would have, if he hadn't known for a fact it was a dead end. The trip back was the hard part.

Alison heard Jake's door close from where she stood by the front window, looking down at the courtyard. She took another sip of tea and then knocked on Billy's door. He told her to come in. He was lying on top of his bed, reading a collection of Raymond Carver stories.

"I just wanted to say thank you," she said. "We left things on the wrong footing just now. I really do appreciate what you did for me out there."

"No problem," he said, setting his book down.

"I hope you can stay, and this all works out," she said. "I guess I'm still getting used to the idea."

"I'll stay if you want me to," he said. "Despite what you might think, you can trust me."

"That's my problem," she said. "I guess I trust the wrong people and distrust the right ones."

He nodded in agreement.

She was about to close the door when she thought of one more thing. "And Billy?"

"Yeah?"

"I'm kind of a modest person. Can you maybe not walk around the apartment in your boxers?"

"Usually I don't even wear these," he said.

"Oh," she said, blushing. "Okay. Keep the boxers.

"Alison," Billy added. "Don't worry about your job. If he threatens you, or whatever, that's sexual harassment. You've got a witness, you know."

"Thanks, Billy," she said. "I appreciate it."

As the morning light began to fill the courtyard, someone stirred in the kitchen of the caretaker's apartment. Jane heard noises, a clattering of dishes, silverware tinkling, but ignored them in favor of ten minutes more sleep. She woke up only when she heard the word "sweetheart" whispered in her ear. When she opened her eyes, she saw that Michael had prepared her breakfast in bed. She saw a tray of muffins, coffee, fresh fruit, and even a rose. It was all so sweet she barely knew what to say.

"Michael," she said. "What's the occasion?" She'd jumped on him the day before for asking what the occasion was, but marriage wasn't about getting even, so he passed on the opportunity.

"You," he said, kissing her.

"What time did you get in last night? I didn't even wake up."

"Some time after three," he said. She sighed. "What is it?"

"I don't know," she said. "We're changing and I don't know into what. At least when we lived in Chicago, I had my family and friends when you were busy. I'm lonely, Michael. I thought people got married to avoid that."

"I know," he said. "I'm trying. We both knew it was going to be tough."

"Tough," Jane said. "It is tough. Very tough."

"Shh," he said, kissing her. "Not this morning. This morning, it's going to be easy." He took the phone off the hook and then kissed her again, running his fingers through her hair, then lightly down her back.

She kissed him fully, whole heartedly, because that was how she loved him, even though it had been more than a week since she'd been able to show it. He wrapped his arms around her and pulled her to him, as somewhere in the building, an alarm went off, and somewhere else in the building, a radio came on, and somewhere else, bacon began to fry in a pan. Jane and Michael heard nothing.

They fell back to sleep and woke up again around eleven o'clock. They could hear sounds coming from the pool through the open window, as Billy wheeled in an old Weber grill he'd found in his parents' garage. Voices talked of an impromptu barbecue. They could hear Rhonda's voice, telling Matt, her best friend, all about her date. From the consoling tone of Matt's voice, it didn't sound like the date had gone well. Then Sandy's voice, shrieking, "Damn you, Jake!" followed by a huge splash as she got thrown in the pool. It was times like these that Los Angeles seemed like a thoroughly livable place, almost a small town. Jane asked Michael if he wanted to go for a swim, adding that it might be nice to cool off.

"Cool off?" he said. "I'm not hot."

"You will be," she whispered, biting him playfully on the earlobe.

6

"LIFE," A COMEDIAN ONCE SAID, "IS JUST high school with money."

"Money," W. Somerset Maugham said, "is like a sixth sense, without which you can't make a complete use of the other five."

"There are four ways to get money," Alison Parker had always said: "you can inherit it, marry it, find it, or earn it." It was too soon to inherit it, and she had no intention of marrying it, though it was her lifelong policy not to turn men down on dates just because they were millionaires. The most money she'd ever found was a twenty-dollar bill, lying on the sidewalk outside the Five & Dime in Eau Claire when she was 14. Like an idiot, she'd turned it over to the cashier, expecting perhaps a reward, or the whole twenty if no one claimed it, but ending up with nothing. The fact was, she knew she'd do the same thing if she found money today, which left only working for it. She remembered another old saying, a line from a poem, though she couldn't remember whose: "heaven protects the working girl." The way her career was going, it was going to take some divine intervention to get her out of the mess she was in.

She was sipping coffee Billy had made when he walked into the kitchen with the morning newspaper.

"This coffee is a little strong," she said, hurrying to make a lunch to take to work.

"I like it that way. It gets my motor running." He rifled through the newspaper as if it was on fire.

She grabbed it from him. "Another thing—I don't want to be picky, but I hate it when someone reads my paper before I do." It drove her crazy, actually. For thirty-five lousy cents, people could buy their own papers.

He snatched the classified ads from her.

"Just need the 'help wanteds,'" he said. "Arthur Murray's okay, but cutting the rug ain't cutting it."

She thumbed through her weekly organizer, then noticed Billy was eating cold pizza for breakfast. People who ate cold pizza for breakfast, she had always thought, should not be allowed to die natural deaths.

"I don't know why I'm in such a rush, they're just going to fire me," she sighed. "I just wish I had somebody to talk to."

"What am I—chopped liver?" he said with his mouth full.

"Somebody from work," she clarified. "To commiserate with."

"Alison, the guy made a pass. He was way out of line. Let him know you're not going to back down. Threaten legal action for sexual harassment. There are laws and he knows it."

"Maybe you're right," she agreed. Billy slapped his finger down on a listing in the want ads.

"Got it," he said, small pieces of cold pizza flying from his face. "Nutritionist."

Downstairs, Michael was opening a jar of roasted red peppers for his omelet with the same set of channel-lock pliers he'd used to fix the toilet in Apartment Seven.

"You know," he said to his wife, "the human cardio-vascular system is a lot like an apartment building's plumbing. Next time I get a myocardial infarction, maybe I'll just go in with one of these." He waved the pliers in air.

"Busy night?" she asked absently.

"Dull as death," he said. "I could rephrase that, but I won't."

"I had a dream this morning," Jane said, out of the blue.

Michael tried to remember his last dream, or even his last good night's sleep. Both eluded him.

"More like a memory. Of the first time we met, that crazy party when I broke my heel and you said you could fix it and then broke the heel off my other shoe. I can still see you standing there with that look on your face, holding my shoes. I knew right then I was in love with you. That very moment."

Michael crossed over to her and put his arms around her.

"I'll break the heels off your new shoes if you want," he said, kissing her on the forehead.

"When was the first time for you?" she asked. "When you knew?"

"When I knew I was in love?" he stalled. She waited for an answer. He saw the look of disappointment cross her face.

"You've forgotten, haven't you?" she said.

"No, I just . . ."

"You've forgotten."

"Come on Jane, that was . . ."

"Two years ago," she said. "Just two."

"Jane," he called after her, but she'd gone into the bedroom to get dressed for work. He'd made a major mistake, and he wasn't sure how to repair the damage. Right now, he had more damage to repair, in the form of a clogged vacuum breaker. Just then there was a knock on the door. It was Jake, wearing only a towel around his waist.

"I've had it with this plumbing, man," Jake said angrily. "I'm in the shower and somebody turns on their hot water, I get frozen. I've been bitching for a month already."

"Not now, Jake," Michael warned him.

"Yeah now," Jake insisted. Michael looked over his shoulder. Jane had disappeared.

"If you're looking to pick a fight, I'm too damn tired."

"All I want to know is, when is it going to be fixed?"

"Well here, Jake," Michael said, offering him the channel lock pliers, "you're out of work, why don't you fix it?"

Matt Fielding had heard the commotion and stepped out of his apartment to intercede. "Take it easy, you guys," Matt said. "It's no big deal."

"I'll call a real plumber, okay, Jake? Happy?"

"Michael," Jane said, at his shoulder now, pulling him away. Rhonda and Alison were descending the courtyard stairs, with Sandy right behind them.

"Just relax about it," Michael told Jake. "I'm getting to it."

"Yeah right," Jake said, walking away.

"Another beautiful day in Lotusland," Rhonda said.

Alison glanced nervously at her watch. "I'm late for work," she said, as Michael closed the door behind him.

Sandy walked around the pool to where Jake stood, trying to calm down but still steamed. He regretted losing his temper with Michael, but he didn't like cold showers either.

"What was that all about?" Sandy asked.

"I dunno. Unemployment blues, maybe."

"I thought you loved the freedom and the lack of responsibilities that come with being out of work," she teased.

"I said that?"

"Something like that."

"Guess I must've grown up," he said. He knew

Sandy was trying to console him, but he didn't want her pity. "I'd better get going. Don't want to keep the unemployment office waiting."

"You'll land on your feet," she said. "Stop by Shooters later and I'll buy you a beer."

"I'll let you," he said. Sandy watched as he hurried across the courtyard toward his apartment.

Late that afternoon, while the bartenders were cutting limes, changing kegs, stocking coolers, and getting ready for the day, Sandy sat on a barstool next to Delia Saldana, the owner of Shooters. Delia was about 50 but looked much younger, full of rock sugar and strong spices, a former actress who'd started her career doing Gerber baby food commercials back when both television and Delia were in their infancies. Later she'd made a number of B movies for Roger Corman, had affairs, it was rumored, with a number of major actors. But then, who in Hollywood, besides the pope, hadn't? And he didn't live in Hollywood. Sandy had asked Delia's opinion of a series of head shots she'd had taken. Delia pored over the photos, trying to think of what to say.

"Kid," Delia said, shaking her head, "none of these airbrush jobs look anything like you."

"That's the point," Sandy said. "I'm trying to show the different sides of myself, my versatility and uniqueness."

"All I see is boobs," Delia said.

"That too," Sandy said. "A girl has to stand out in this town."

"Talent is what's going to set you apart from the rest," Delia promised. "Now get to work, Meryl Streep. Tonight you play the role of waitress."

"What's my motivation?" Sandy Stanislawskied.

"I'll fire your behind, that's your motivation," Delia answered her. Sandy turned, to find Kelly standing behind her, apparently waiting for an opportunity to interrupt.

"Kelly," Sandy said in greeting.

"I was looking for Jake," Kelly said.

"As usual . . ."

"I wanted to tell him Jackie had her baby."

"That Jake sure gets around, don't he?" Sandy surmised.

"Jackie is my mother," Kelly corrected.

"You call your mother 'Jackie?'" Sandy asked, amazed. "I call mine 'Mother.' 'Ma'am' if I've been bad. So, you got a new baby in the family. I guess they'll have to pay the babysitter extra now."

"Just tell me if he's here," Kelly demanded coolly.

"He's down at the unemployment office, darlin'," Sandy said. "They don't have those in Beverly Hills." She scrinched her face at Kelly and sauntered toward a cluttered table.

Thoughts of the unemployment office had crossed Alison's mind as she parked her car that morning in the parking lot next to D&D Advertising. She found Hal Barber standing alone in the reception area, presumably checking the mail, though she had the sense he was lying in wait for her. For once, she'd been glad traffic on the freeway was slow, because it had given her a chance to practice what she was going to say to him. She saw no reason to postpone the inevitable, and approached him. When he saw her, he smiled. The smile she'd once thought sincere, though now she could see how phony it was.

"Alison," he began.

"I know you're busy," she interrupted, "but this won't take long. What happened the other night between us was sexual harassment, plain and simple. There are several ways I could take this, charges I could bring. I want you to know I've considered all the options, and if it means losing my job, so be it. What I'm saying is, I will not be intimidated."

"Alison," he said, "we went out. We had a date."

"It was more than that."

"Okay, maybe I was out of line," he said, sneering at her. "It won't happen again."

"Not after I file charges, it won't," she replied.

"Do what you want," he said. He walked off without looking back, as arrogant as he'd been the first time she'd met him. Why didn't she trust her first impressions?

She was still staring angrily at the space where Hal had stood, when someone approached her from behind, a secretary from another department who tapped her on the shoulder and said she couldn't help overhearing.

"Apparently you haven't heard," the secretary said. "Libby Haskins in payroll already filed charges. Hal Barber is dead."

Amazed, Alison let the news sink in. "Well what

do you know," she said. "There is a God. Maybe we could all get together and file a class action suit."

"You're Alison Parker, right?" Alison nodded. "In that case, your cab is here."

"My cab?" Alison said. "I didn't call a cab."

A big yellow Checker taxi waited at the curb. Alison stepped past the tinted glass doors and into the sunshine. She walked to the cab and leaned down to speak to the driver.

It was Billy.

"Oh my God," Alison said. "You stole a cab."

"It's perfect," he said, getting out to give her a better view, as if she'd never seen the inside of a cab before. "Welcome to my new job. This'll pay twice what teaching dance did."

"Billy . . ."

"Come on, Alison. This is a big opportunity for me. I get a piece of the action, plus tips, and I'm my own boss. Plus, think of all the stories I'll be able to collect for my writing. It's great! I just came by to see if you wanted to celebrate tonight."

"I had plans to paint the apartment," she said. "Michael's going to have the paint ready for me when I get home."

"Then we'll paint it together," he said. "The brushes, the rollers, the toxic fumes, I love painting."

It was fun to see him so filled with enthusiasm.

"Geez, I forgot! How'd it go with your jerk boss?"

"Hoisted by his own petard," she said with satisfaction.

"Ouch," Billy winced. "That happened to me once in high school—hurts like a sonofabitch."

Just then, the radio cackled, summoning him to a fare across town. "Roger wilco Houston, over and out," he said into the mike. "Is this a great job or what? See you tonight—you bring the paint and I'll get the beer. Painting without beer is like . . . well, like anything else without beer." With that, he peeled away from the curb, his tires squealing.

Jake Hanson was not in nearly as good a mood. The fluorescent-lit, linoleum-floored unemployment office was about as cozy as an empty filing cabinet. He sat on a bench that had ridges nailed onto the seat every twenty-four inches, to prevent people from lying down or napping. Above him, a fluorescent light flickered and buzzed. There were over a hundred men and women in the room, all waiting for their names to be called by one of three social service officers. Finally Jake heard his name called. He went to window two, where he faced a man who looked like he hadn't smiled since World War II. Jake tried to make small talk.

"Crowded today."

"Lots of people out of work," the officer said with a satisfied air, like a mortician happy to note business is good. He read the forms Jake had filled out and handed them back. "The instructions clearly state you have to fill out the boxes on the left and right side. Finish this and take it to window C for re-submission."

"I started at window C," Jake protested.

"McBride," the officer said into the microphone, already moving on to the next case. Jake felt his temperature start to rise.

* * *

Billy was having somewhat better luck. He'd had four fares already that morning, including a businessman on an expense account coming from LAX who'd tipped him ten bucks for a twenty-dollar ride. He hadn't gotten lost once. He was thinking of breaking for lunch, maybe a chili dog with sauerkraut at Ed's Eats, his favorite diner, when he saw a woman waving a scarf in the air. She was cute, early twenties, dressed in a job-interview suit, with the kind of legs you read about in books, and a bewildered look on her face. When she got in the cab, she told him it was in the Valley.

"What's in the Valley?"

"Where I'm going. I've never been there. Do you know where it is?"

"The Valley? Born and bred," he said. She handed him a piece of paper with an address on it. He looked at it. "No problem. We'll find it." He looked in the rearview mirror. He could be wrong, but the way she smiled at him, he could have sworn she liked him.

"That's the problem with this town," he was saying, ten minutes later, "too many people and nobody's from here." He'd been blathering since he'd picked her up, but she was loving it, laughing and asking him questions, the best fare he'd had so far. "Everybody's so transient, it's like a built-in escape clause in the social contract, screw thy neighbor—why not? You'll never see each other again." He made a mental note to use that image in his writing, some day. "We got, like, six million total strangers, and they like it that way.

That's what I don't get. If you want to be left alone, why move to the biggest city in the country? It makes no sense. Am I talking too much?"

"No, I like it," she told him. "It's true what you're saying. You never meet anyone who's real."

"Exactly," he said, pulling up to a stop light. "It's like a whole city, afraid of commitment." He glanced in the rearview mirror when he heard the rear door open and close and was completely surprised when the woman got in the front seat with him.

"You don't mind do you?" she said, offering her hand. "Marcy Garrett."

"Not at all," he said, shaking her hand. "Billy Campbell." She was staring at him. "What?"

"Nothing," she said. "You just . . . you look like Bruce Springsteen."

"Me?" he said, flattered. "Get out."

"No, you do, back when he had an edge. I saw him at the Coliseum."

"The 'Born in the USA' tour? I was there," he said, suddenly excited to think that it had to be more than just a coincidence, fate had thrown them together. Fate did stuff like that. Especially with writers.

"Saturday night."

"Me, too."

"Tenth row, on the field."

"Twelfth row," she said. "My God, we were two rows apart."

"We could've danced in the aisles together," he said. They looked deeply into each other's eyes. Billy'd had a hunch the day he moved out of his parents' house that he was going to fall in love soon, but he never expected to meet anybody this way. "Look, this is crazy, but I know an Italian place up on Mulholland where we could get some lunch . . ."

"I love Italian food," she replied. It was incredible. He'd never met a girl who'd given him so many green lights.

"Green light," she said.

"I beg your pardon."

"The light," she said. "It's changed. You can go."

At the unemployment office, Jake was approaching the front of the line at window C, waiting only for a second social services officer to finish dealing with a Latino woman with a small child in her arms. This bureaucratic geek was worse than the first, a tall, greasy-haired 40-year-old goon with skin like the belly of a fish. For ten minutes, he'd been withholding the woman's check because of some petty detail. Jake couldn't help but eavesdrop.

"No madam," the officer was saying, "we have to reissue the check to your new address."

"Please, *señor. Mi esposo, no esté trabajando.* We need check today." The check had already been filled out, and sat on the counter before her.

"I can't do that," the man said. "It's the policy."

"Come on man," Jake said, "just give her the check."

"Are you with this woman?" the goon asked imperviously.

"I'm her friend," Jake said, approaching the

window.

"Well then explain to your friend here that, because she's changed addresses, there's a two-week waiting period."

"That's crazy! You've got it right there." He pointed toward the check on the other side of the window.

"Next," the man called out.

"I'm next," Jake said. The officer was gesturing to the man behind Jake. The woman was beginning to cry. The child had already started wailing. Jake reached across the counter, grabbed the check and handed it to the woman.

"Hey you can't do that," the goon protested.

"Here you go," Jake told the woman. "Go. Take off, *vamos*."

"*Gracias, señor,*" she said.

The officer came running around the counter and grabbed Jake by the arm. Angry beyond reason, Jake shook his arm loose and pushed the geek into the crowd of people waiting, none of whom made any effort to catch the officer, who fell heavily to the ground. Jake heard the crowd cheer as three other security guards set upon him. More shouting.

Cursing, he broke free of one of the guards, at which point he noticed a blond girl standing at the edge of the action. It was Kelly.

"What are you doing here?" he asked her, his efforts to break free of his captors lapsing.

"What did you do? Leave him alone, you're hurting him," he heard Kelly shout, but then he was wrestled into a back room by the guards, and completely lost sight of her.

7

AT THE LOCAL POLICE STATION, KELLY found herself surrounded by exactly the sort of people her mother had warned her all her life she'd encounter (and possibly become one of) if she didn't finish her vegetables, clean her room, and walk the straight and narrow path; criminals and panhandlers, winos and prostitutes, killers and thieves, and a pair of local politicians in the corner giving some sort of news conference. She'd tried to pay Jake's bail with her gold card, but now the desk cop, a pleasant enough young woman, was handing her back her plastic.

"Afraid you're over your limit, miss," the cop said. "They're not accepting it."

"There must be some mistake." She couldn't be

out of credit—she hadn't been to Rodeo Drive in
months.

"There are half a dozen bail bondsmen across
the street . . ."

"They told me they need collateral," she
explained. "A thousand dollars seems so high."

"Mr. Hanson created a disturbance at a state
agency," the desk cop said. "With his priors, you're
lucky it's not five."

"What's a 'prior?'" Kelly's brown eyes filled
with worry.

"Prior arrests," the cop explained. "Your
boyfriend has led a colorful life."

Billy turned the key to his apartment door to
find it dark inside. He turned on the lights and then
stepped aside, bidding Marcy to enter.

"My humble abode," he said, his arm sweeping
wide. She looked around.

"It's great," she said. Billy wondered what she
made of all of Alison's feminine touches, but didn't
choose to explain. Having babes over was exactly
what he'd had in mind when he moved in, and
nothing was going to spoil it.

"Strawberries?" he offered, picking up a fruit
bowl from the table.

She said she would love one.

He suggested they sit on the couch, where they
would be more comfortable.

When she sat down, he sat next to her and fed her
a plump juicy strawberry. He had to admire the way

she ate it, fearlessly and with great enthusiasm. They found themselves face-to-face, the room suddenly silent.

"Well, here we are," she said.

"Here we are," he said. "Two rows apart."

"And closing," she said. "We should be careful."

"I know."

"I can't help myself."

"Me neither," he said, and then they kissed. Billy briefly thought he shouldn't try to break any world records with this, his very first kiss in his new apartment, out in the world at large, away from home. But then, records were made to be broken. It would give him something to shoot for. For her part, Marcy kissed as if she wanted to exchange teeth. She had one hand on the back of his neck, one hand caressing his face and another on his belt buckle. He didn't know how she was doing it, but he didn't want her to stop. Then someone walked in.

Alison.

"Billy?"

"My God," Marcy said, "you've got a girlfriend."

"No I don't," he told her.

"Roommate," Alison said, feeling embarrassed and little stunned. She waved hello. "Strictly platonic. Barely even that."

The girl on the couch brushed her hair back and smiled, introducing herself as Marcy.

Billy explained that he'd just met her in the cab.

"The cab," Alison said.

"I told you it was a great job," Billy said.

"It's just so wacky," Marcy babbled. "I mean, of all the guys I know . . . I meet . . . I mean, I've met, and then this guy just drives up . . ."

"It's unbelievable," Billy said, shaking his head. "Totally."

"It certainly is," Alison said, a fake I'm-so-happy-for-you smile plastered across her face. It was only then that Billy noticed Alison was carrying two gallons of paint she'd picked up from Michael's apartment. "Look," she said, "would you like me to come back later?"

"Oh no," Marcy said. "I don't want to inconvenience you."

"No, we can get out of your way," Billy offered.

"You can show me your bedroom," Marcy said, her eyes sparkling with promise.

"There's not much to see."

"In that case we can leave the light off," she said, giggling.

It wasn't so much the fact that Billy had a girl over, while Alison hadn't had a date in months—not counting the party with Hal. Nor was it the fact that Billy had promised to help her paint and now she had to do it all alone. Alison could handle that. It was the fact that some people seemed to lead charmed lives, while hers was cursed, that drove her out of her mind sometimes.

Alison changed into her overalls, poured the paint in the roller pan, and spread a drop cloth, intending to start in the hallway. She heard noises coming from Billy's room. She looked for her Walkman, then frowned as she remembered that her batteries were dead. More noises, giggles, squeals. Marcy saying, "Gee Billy, I swear this isn't like me, I'm serious," followed by heavy sighs and moans of delight. It sounded, as Alison pressed her ear against Billy's door, as if they were playing tackle football in there, things crashing and spilling, furniture moving around, grunts and groans. The door opened.

"Oh, hi Billy," Alison said, backing away from the door, caught red-handed. "I was just . . . uh . . . painting the hall."

"Oh. Are we bothering you?"

"No, not at all . . . it's just . . . the walls are thin."

"Maybe a new coat of paint will help," he said. She grabbed his arm and pulled him into the living room, speaking in a fierce whisper.

"Have you lost your mind?" she asked him. "You just met this woman—you don't know her. She's just a . . ."

"Fare?"

"A fare," Alison agreed. "And she has a very strange idea of tipping. I mean, my God, Billy, you should at least—"

"Use condoms?"

"No!" Alison said. "I mean yes. I wasn't referring to that."

"We're bothering you. I can tell."

"Look, I don't want to get into this."

"What is it? What's the problem?"

"There's no problem. I'm just . . . we were going to paint." From the bedroom, they could hear Marcy, calling for Billy.

"No sweat. I'll help you tomorrow," Billy said, as he backed toward his door.

"If you could just keep it down, somehow," Alison pleaded.

"I've got just the solution," he said, returning to his room. Moments later, Alison heard the stereo in Billy's room blasting Bruce Springsteen, singing "Born In the USA." She doubted Billy was teaching Marcy how to tango.

The next morning, Alison was eating a bowl of Cheerios at the kitchen table in her painting overalls when Marcy stumbled out of Billy's room, asking if she could borrow Alison's deodorant, explaining that she hadn't really been prepared. Not missing a beat, Marcy returned to the bathroom. Just then Billy dragged himself into the kitchen scratching his stomach, and popped a bagel into the toaster. He looked about half awake. They said nothing to each other while the bagel toasted. Finally Billy spoke.

"Nothing happened," he said. "We just talked."

Alison sighed. "I didn't ask," she said, feigning indifference.

"You seem relieved," Billy said with a smirk. "We should talk about these feelings of yours."

"I'm not having any feelings," Alison said defensively. Marcy returned and asked if she could have a grapefruit. Alison grudgingly obliged. Marcy, seeing Alison in paint-splattered overalls two times in a row, asked her if she painted apartments for a living. Marcy was, Alison surmised, not too bright. When Billy asked Marcy what she did for a living—apparently they'd talked all night and never gotten around to the subject—Marcy told Billy to guess.

"Teacher?" he said. She shook her head, giggling at the fun game she'd invented. "Lawyer?"

"Better," Marcy said. "Come on Alison, you guess too."

"Astronaut?" Alison said. "Brain surgeon?

"Close," Marcy said.

"Heiress?" Billy said wishfully. "Tycoon? Tycoon-ess?"

"Dental student!" Marcy shrieked.

Alison suppressed a laugh when she saw how impressed Billy was.

"Wow," he said. "That's fantastic."

"I'll be at the paint store. They mixed the wrong colors," Alison said, rising and dumping her cereal bowl in the sink; she made a beeline for the door.

Across the street from the paint store was a bank. Kelly Taylor stood in line there, accompanied by her friend Donna. When she got to the window, Kelly handed the teller a savings account withdrawal slip for a thousand dollars. Donna rolled her eyes.

"This is so totally beyond crazy," Donna said. "That's your spending money for Europe."

"I know what I'm doing," Kelly said.

"Come on, Kel. Arrested? And he's been arrested before? Dylan told you the guy was trouble."

"Donna, it's not that big a deal."

"How do you know? It could be anything." Kelly stuffed the bills into her purse, more cash than she'd ever carried in her life and strode toward the revolving door. Donna raced to keep up with her.

"Isn't your car the other way?" Kelly said.

"Jake could get you in big trouble," Donna warned.

"When you love someone, you don't care about things like that," Kelly said. "I'd do anything for Jake."

"Then you're saying this is, like, actually and truly love?"

"Yes," Kelly told her friend. "That's what I'm saying." She got into her car and started the engine. Donna was saying that Kelly shouldn't run crying to her for sympathy when she got her heart broken, but Kelly had an urgent appointment to keep at the police station.

She was waiting in the hallway when a guard buzzed Jake through a security door, handing him his wallet and keys from a manila envelope. She ran to him and threw her arms around him, relieved that nothing had happened to him in jail.

"I'm sorry it took so long," she told him, "but I had to wait for the bank to open."

"You bailed me out?" he asked.

"Well, yeah . . ."

"Look," he said angrily, "you shouldn't have gotten involved."

"I had to," she said. "You were in trouble."

"When are you going to figure it out?" he said. "I'm no good for you. You're from a different world than me."

"But I understand you, Jake. I know what you're feeling."

He stared at her, his teeth clenched. It couldn't go on like this. How could she understand him when he didn't understand himself?

"I'll pay you back as soon as I can," he said, heading for the door. He heard her calling after him, "Jake, please don't do this . . ." but he just kept on walking.

8

ALISON PARKER RAN SOME ERRANDS, DID some window shopping, bought a birthday card for her mother, thought long and hard about changing her hairstyle, had her oil changed at a Jiffylube, treated herself to dinner out at an inexpensive but nice Mexican restaurant Matt had recommended, and came home to find the apartment awash in candle glow. Marcy sat cozily on the couch, reading a copy of *Vogue* magazine, moving her lips. She looked up, startled.

"Oh. Hi, Alison," she said. "I was expecting Billy."

"I assumed," Alison replied.

"He's at the grocery store. He's going to make me dinner."

"What a guy."

"He is, isn't he? I think he's swell," Marcy said. Alison was more concerned with the lighted candle Marcy had placed on top of a gallon of turpentine. She blew the candle out.

"Flammable," she explained, tapping the tin container.

"You must think I'm impulsive," Marcy said. "I'm as blown away as you are. Normally I live a very structured organized life. Lately I've had all this pressure from exams at school, and then I met Billy, and . . ." Marcy had to stop to catch her breath. "We just had this instant attraction, and the next thing I knew, I wanted to be with him every second of every day. You've got to tell me everything you know about him—what he likes, doesn't like, his old girlfriends, everything."

"Actually I don't think I can be much help," Alison said, trying to decide if she should go to plan B and paint her bedroom instead of the kitchen. "He only moved in a week ago."

"Really?" Marcy said. "I'm surprised. For someone you've known such a short time, you're very protective."

"Am I?" Alison said, worried that she might be giving that impression.

Marcy said, "yes, you really are."

"Listen," Alison said, "I'm the last person you need to feel threatened by."

"Threatened?" Marcy said. "Who says I feel threatened?"

Billy entered, carrying a bag of groceries in each

arm, dinner for two, coming up. He smiled good-naturedly and greeted them, only to be attacked by Marcy, who leapt across the room and kissed him so hard her tongue seemed about to start coming out his ears.

"Welcome home, Billy," Marcy cooed, slobbering and fawning over him like a dog.

Alison shot Billy a glance to say, Billy, this is sick and you know it.

Marcy took the groceries, giggling and thrilled, and started unpacking, examining each item and reading the labels out loud.

"Why don't we eat later?" Billy proposed.

"Later," she said with a grin, catching his drift. "After we've worked up an appetite." She pulled him by the hand and dragged him into the bedroom, Billy barely managing an "excuse us" before disappearing into Marcy's clutches.

Alison sat at the kitchen table, wondering what to do, until she noticed that one of the grocery bags Billy had brought home had moved. She sat up, keeping her eye on it. It moved again. She was sure. She was reaching for the bag, wondering what in the world could be inside it, when it suddenly jumped and fell over. She stifled a scream and stepped back as a huge lobster crawled out of the bag, its antennae feeling the air.

Well, Alison thought. At least I've got some company for the evening.

Michael had brought home a pizza for dinner, hoping it would mollify Jane somehow. For all the things he knew how to fix where the human body was concerned, sometimes it still astonished him how little there was he knew how to do to fix a relationship. He usually did stupid, male things like buy Jane roses or chocolates, when he knew their problems went far deeper than any candy or flower could reach. It was as if a physician were to say, nurse, this patient is having a heart attack — quick, change the bedsheets. Jane had been brooding all day.

"Come on, Jane," he urged. "Talk to me."

"I know I shouldn't be this angry," she said. "If forgetting the first time you knew you loved me was the only issue, I'd agree, I'm being unreasonable, but I think this whole thing is symptomatic of a bigger problem."

"I didn't say you were being unreasonable," he said. "Let's just discuss it. And not panic."

"But we should panic," Jane said. "If the romance in our relationship is dead, we should be terrified."

As usual, before they could finish their business, there was a knock on the door.

Michael got it. It was Alison. He told her if she was complaining about the plumbing, he would have it fixed tomorrow before what was becoming the weekly barbecue. She walked in without being invited.

"I wish the plumbing was my only problem," she steamed. "You've met Marcy of course, Billy's new girlfriend. Girlfriend! The speed those two are traveling, she's probably his fiancée by now. They think they're in love and they've known each other all of twenty-four hours. Maybe I'm just a

cheesehead from Wisconsin, but are all relation-
ships in L.A. this ridiculous?"

"Maybe it's love at first sight," Jane offered.

"You believe in love at first sight?"

"Yes, I do," Jane said, looking at Michael.

"For some people, it's more gradual," Michael
told Alison, looking at Jane. "So you're here
because you're worried about Billy?"

"I've been driven out of my apartment!" Alison
sputtered. "The incessant giggling, the mooning, the
endless 'Born in the USA, Born in the USA,' over
and over. Twenty-four hours and they have their
own theme song."

"You have your own bedroom, don't you?"
Michael said.

"I know. I'm just . . ."

"Jealous?" Jane guessed.

"Why does everyone assume that?" Alison
asked. "We're just roommates, and maybe even
friends. But now . . . I hate being treated like I'm
not there. Like I don't count. I'd talk to him about
it but he's too busy playing spank and tickle to hear
me. I really shouldn't be this upset." She took several deep breaths, trying to calm down.

"Slap and tickle," Michael said, correcting her.

"Whatever."

"What can we do for you?" Jane asked sympa-
thetically.

"Can I stay here tonight, on your couch?"
Alison pleaded. "You two have it so together . . ."

Michael and Jane exchanged glances.

Thomas Calabro as apartment manager/intern Michael Mancini.

Josie Bisset as up-and-coming fashion designer Jane Mancini.

Andrew Shue as the irresistible and irrepressible Billy Campbell.

Courtney Thorne-Smith as the ambitious and creative Alison Parker.

Amy Locane as the sultry beauty Sandy Harling.

Grant Show as the resident loner Jake Hanson.

Doug Savant as social worker Matt Fielding.

Vanessa Williams as hot aerobics instructor Rhonda Blair.

Andrew Shue and Courtney Thorne-Smith as roommates Billy Campbell and Alison Parker.

"To friendship." Andrew Shue as Billy Campbell, Grant Show as Jake Hanson, Doug Savant as Matt Fielding.

*   *   *

At the barbecue the next day, all was merriment and mirth, to the tune of "Born in the USA," of course, playing from the stereo Billy had brought poolside.

Marcy seemed to have found a friend in Matt. "This is so cool, the way you all know each other," she gushed. "In my building, we're all strangers."

"It's a nice place," Matt agreed. "We look out for each other."

"Kind of like a family."

By the barbecue, Rhonda was telling Billy he flipped a mean burger. Talent passed along in the family genes, Billy explained.

Rhonda thought it was hilarious to see Billy so head over heels and Matt stopped by the grill to tell Billy he liked Marcy, adding, "she says what's on her mind. You got lucky, Billy-boy, she's nuts about you."

Off to the side, Sandy was giving head shots to Steve Sanders, Kelly's friend with the famous actress mother, asking him his opinion of each.

"These are terrific," he told Sandy, pointing to several photos.

"I studied at Actors' Circle and six months with Charles Nelson Reilly," Sandy said, hoping Steve would take the hint. "All I need are a few credits on there . . ."

"I love this low-cut number," he said, holding a photograph up to the light. "By the way, great party."

"I'm glad you're enjoying yourself," she told him.

"Listen, next week my friends and I are having

a little party down at the beach club."

"Come on Steve, a high school party? You promised you'd take me to Hollywood parties. You know, with agents? Producers?"

"Who wants to go to one of those?" Steve asked.

"I do," Sandy growled.

"Hello," Marcy said, coming over to introduce herself. "I'm Marcy. I'm Billy's lover."

Sandy rolled her eyes.

"I can say that, can't I?"

"Not around me," Steve said with a grin. "I'm in high school."

Sandy caught Jake on his way to his apartment, shunning the party in progress. He paused when he heard Sandy call his name.

"You never let me buy you that beer," Sandy reminded him.

"I've been busy," he said.

She wagged her eyebrows lasciviously.

"Butt out, Sandy."

"Did I say anything?"

Billy found a free lounge chair next to Jane and sat down to eat his burger, a half-pound of extra lean, medium rare, on a toasted sesame bun, a beer at his side. The only way life could get any better than this, he thought, would be if Cindy Crawford were in the room next door, doing his laundry. He looked at Marcy. She was pretty cool too.

"Remember everything that happens today," Jane told Billy, glancing at Michael. "Etch it in your memory. Falling in love is the greatest experience a person can have."

"Burger, Jane?" Billy asked, trying to get her to lighten up a little. "You think this is love?"

"What else?" As Marcy and Rhonda walked by, Billy could hear Marcy telling Rhonda how cute she thought it was that he wore socks to bed. He asked Jane to excuse him and went to talk to Alison, who was manning the grill. She handed him the spatula.

"You avoiding me?" he asked her. "I haven't seen you around."

"You've had your mind on other things," Alison said.

"It's really weird," Billy confessed. "It all happened so fast, getting a new job, then Marcy, now this, introducing her to my friends and spending every second together. Don't tell anybody, but this is the first real adult affair I've ever had."

"She's the most aggressive woman I've ever met," Alison conceded.

"I had a feeling you didn't like her," he said.

"Liking her has nothing to do with it," Alison said. "I just think it's strange, the way she's glommed onto you. She's telling everybody about your whole sex life."

"Look, just because I rescued you from Hal doesn't mean you need to rescue me from Marcy," Billy said defensively.

"Did I say you needed rescuing?" Alison said smugly. "Must be your own perception, Billy-boy." Across the pool, Marcy was telling Sandy and Rhonda about how quickly he'd learned just how to touch her. He suddenly imagined turning on a television and seeing Marcy as a guest on Dr. Ruth

Westheimer's show, today's theme, "vimin who kent get enuff zex—zo Marcy, tell us about Beely."

"Well," Marcy told the whole world, including Billy's parents, "no man has ever satisfied me like Billy, and I'm notoriously over-sexed. He had this way of using his fingers . . ."

"Billy," he heard from somewhere outside his hallucination. "Billy! The burgers are burning." It was Rhonda, bringing him back to reality. "I'll take over," she said, giving him a knowing glance. "You're going to save up your strength for tonight."

That night, Marcy was in the kitchen fixing a snack while Billy watched television on the couch— a close-up of a female black widow spider. An announcer with a British accent was describing how, after mating, the female becomes aggressive and then stuns, kills and devours the male. He flipped through the channels. *Fatal Attraction* was on cable. He turned the television off.

Marcy joined Billy on the couch with another bowl of strawberries, and tried to feed him one. This time, Billy didn't feel like strawberries.

"I can't believe tomorrow is already Monday," she said.

"Didn't you say you had an exam?"

"Tomorrow," she laughed. "I haven't even studied."

"There's still tonight," he suggested.

"But it's Sunday . . ."

"I've got some writing I wanted to do," he said. "We've been together all weekend."

"I know. It's been great. I love your friends."

"They like you, too. But, your exam, and my writing—"

"You've got your whole life to write, and I've got my whole life to be a dentist," she said, cozying up. "This is the magic time, Billy." She kissed him.

He kissed her back. For now, anyway.

She broke it off to tell him something. "Billy?"

"Yeah?"

"I can't."

"Tell me."

"Billy, I think I love you," she said. Billy tried to reply, but the only sound he could manage was a guttural "urrgp."

"I know," Marcy said, nodding. "Don't try to speak."

In the courtyard, Michael was working on the plumbing, but he was having a hard time getting a grip with the pipe wrench. Night was coming on, and he had a utility light hanging from the branch of a large ficus tree nearby. He heard footsteps and looked up to see Jake, holding his motorcycle helmet in his hand.

"Missed a good barbecue," Michael told Jake.

"What are you up to?" Jake asked, kneeling down.

"I wish I knew," Michael admitted.

"You got rust there," Jake said, taking a can of

penetrating oil from the tool box. He took the
wrench from Michael after applying the oil, and
soon worked the pipe free. He pointed to the tool
box. "That saw's not going to make it."

"Only one I've got," Michael said.

"First let's get this plaster out of the way," Jake
said, taking off his jacket, "then I'll get mine."
Together, they set about replacing the faulty pipe. Jake
paused a moment. "Sorry about the other morning."

"Don't worry about it," Michael said.

"Sometimes I don't deal with things too well."

"You've got a lot of friends here, Jake. You can
ask for help if you need it."

"Where I come from, you pull your own weight."

"I come from the same place," Michael said.
"Macho land."

"I'll get my saw," Jake said. While he waited,
Michael looked back to his apartment, where he
saw Jane standing in the open door. She waved
good night to him, then turned and closed the door
behind her. He knew he should drop what he was
doing and go to her, but he couldn't. His whole life
was like that, responsibilities at cross purposes.

The next morning, Alison was eating breakfast
and glancing at the paper when Billy came in.

"Quiet this morning," she said without looking
up. "She gone?"

"Look," Billy said, hoping Alison could help
him. "I don't need this from you right now. I have a
real problem here. She's in love with me."

"Congratulations."

"No, I mean, she's really in love with me."

"Well of course she's in love with you," Alison said, putting down the paper. "Billy, you invited her into your life. What did you expect?"

"Look, I thought it was love, too," he said. "In the beginning. But after a few nights . . . I was in lust, not love."

"Billy," Alison said. "I'm not interested in this." Billy stared out the window for a moment.

"Well we're sure some pair, aren't we?" he said, heading for the bathroom.

"What does that mean?"

"The other morning you said you wished you had someone to talk to," he reminded her. "Now when I need somebody . . ."

"Billy!" Marcy called from the bathroom. "I need a towel."

"In a minute!" he called back.

Alison had to get to work. She felt sorry for Billy, but she'd already tried to warn him.

As Alison started her car, Jake roared past her on his motorcycle. In a few minutes, he'd left Melrose Place far behind him and was cruising along the smooth, palm-lined streets of Beverly Hills, past the mansions and past the tourists peering up at the mansions through binoculars, hoping to catch a glimpse of somebody important or famous, as if it could make their own lives important or famous somehow. Jake was part of a sizable minority in Los Angeles who hated celebrities and wished they'd all go away. Jake didn't feel comfortable in Beverly Hills either, but today he had a visit he had to make. When he turned into Kelly's driveway, he saw her standing with her stepbrother David. He stopped the motorcycle short of the house and waited for Kelly to come to him. When she got there, he handed her an envelope containing the money he'd gotten from his unemployment check.

"There's two hundred there," he said. "I'll give you the rest when I've got it." She didn't say anything. "Okay?"

"Is that what you want me to say?" Kelly asked. "Okay?"

"I'm just trying to even the score."

"It's not about money."

"I don't like being in debt."

"I was helping you."

"And now you want something in return," he said. That was how people from Beverly Hills thought, wasn't it? Life was a series of deals, emotional and otherwise.

"Wrong," Kelly said. "I could care less. My God. You're always making such a big deal about me being the kid, when it's you who's acting like one." She threw the envelope at him. "Keep your money."

He let the envelope lie where it fell. She ran back to the house, upset again. He gunned the throttle, spun the rear tire around on the blacktop and sped away, feeling the need for a long fast ride to clear his head. There were no answers on the road, but sometimes if you rode fast enough, you could forget the questions.

BILLY WAS FEELING LIKE A JERK, OR LIKE someone who had the potential of soon becoming a jerk, and since Alison didn't seem to want to talk about it, he figured the next best thing would be to talk to somebody else who was already a jerk, or at least someone who was widely regarded as such, which meant Jake, though in Billy's limited experience, Jake had been nothing but straightforward and decent. The crowd at Shooters was mostly the diehards, the people who would be there on their own birthdays. He spotted Jake at the bar, where he appeared to be trying to melt a bottle of Budweiser with X-ray vision. Sandy was filling in behind the bar, and smiled as Billy sat on the stool next to Jake.

"Whatever he's having," Billy told Sandy, turning to Jake. "How's the job search going?"

"It's not," Jake said. He sounded surly. "Something you want to talk about?"

"Where's Marcy, Billy?" Sandy interrupted. "She give you the night off?"

"Something like that," Billy said, turning his shoulder to let Sandy know this was just between him and Jake. "The subject is women," he said to Jake. "Your specialty."

"Not today man," Jake said.

"But this is right up your alley," Billy persisted. "You meet a girl, things develop, you sleep with her, she falls in love with you, and then you're hosed. You like her, but it's not love, and you're not ready for anything serious. What do you do?"

Jake looked at Billy a moment longer, then burst out laughing.

Billy ignored it. "I'm thinking I'll just avoid her," Billy said. "What do you think? Maybe a little bogus?"

Jake thought this would be a perfect time for Kelly to come looking for him again. "I wouldn't recommend it," he told Billy. "Hiding is okay, if you want to just hang out, listen to music, hit on strangers. And this is the place for it, but no way is it a solution."

"It works for you," Billy said.

Jake became completely serious. "Tell me what in my life is working right now?" he wanted to know. "You can put up a macho front thinking, hey, I'm cool, I can handle it. But you're not being straight with people. If it's not working out, or she's crowding you, then you gotta tell her. Say you've got other priorities, or you gotta work on your career and the timing is all wrong, or just tell her it's not love. You owe her that." He finished his beer and set it down on the bar. "And admit it's your fault, too. You must have come on pretty strong to her."

"I did," Billy said, which was exactly why he felt so guilty. Jake asked him if he wanted to play pool, but he said he had too much on his mind, and wanted to take a walk.

Sandy picked up the money Billy had left on the bar.

"Doctor Jake," she mocked. "The man who has a solution to everyone's problems but his own."

"You busy tonight?" Jake asked her.

"Why? You askin' me out?" she said, leaning against the beer coolers.

"Something like that."

"Three's a crowd."

"I was thinking of just the two of us."

"Were you?" she said, smiling to herself in a way that said 'not even in his dreams.' Her answer was not unexpected. Many are cold, he thought, watching her walk away from him, but few are frozen.

When Billy got home, Marcy was waiting for him, greeting him like he'd just gone to the North Pole and back. To make matters worse, she'd baked him a loaf of bread and written his name on the top of the loaf in raisins. She told him how worried she'd gotten when he hadn't called her at lunchtime.

"We've got to talk," he said.

"I know," she said. "So much has happened so fast—"

"No, I mean, really talk—"

"Nothing like this has ever happened to me, Billy, I mean, I've had other men in my life and I know it's only been a few days, but it really feels like love—"

"Marcy, please," Billy said, grabbing her by the arms. The way she looked at him, he knew she knew what was coming. "This thing is . . . it's totally out of control. You're coming on so strong."

"So were you," she said. "At first. I was just being honest, about my feelings."

"Marcy—we've known each other two days— how can you know it's love?" he asked.

"How do you know it isn't?" she asked him back.

"Well that's it then," he said. "It's not a provable thing. It's just how you feel. I don't feel the same way you do. I don't love you."

A single tear rolled slowly down her cheek. "Why do I always do this?" she asked. "I meet somebody, and then I just lose control, and I'm all over them until I drive them away. I don't know how to take my time."

Billy decided not to point out that just minutes earlier, she'd been saying how nothing like this had ever happened to her before. "Marcy, I'm sorry."

"Forget it," she said, sniffing and brushing away the tear. "Look, I'll be okay. God, I hate this part." She broke away from him and picked up her books. "I've got to get home and study anyway."

There was nothing Billy could say. He almost asked her if he could call her a taxi.

Before she left, she stopped and turned to him. "You know," she said, "maybe I'm crazy, but Alison . . . you and her . . . I've got a feeling. Well, anyway, see you Billy."

Jane was standing at her apartment window, looking out at the courtyard as Marcy walked past with tears running down her cheeks. Jane didn't know whether to feel relieved or sorry. Every failed romance seemed like another blow against the empire of love. But then, it would be unrealistic to hope that every relationship would end in bliss. Maybe it was unrealistic to hope that any relationship would. Michael was at the dining room table, catching up on reading medical journals. She went to him and rubbed his shoulders.

"I'm, sorry," she said. "I've been a real jerk lately."

"I deserved it," he said. "I'm serious. You made me think of some things. I don't want to lose the romance either, you know."

"So we won't, that's all," she said. "What do you want for dinner? I've got some left-over pasta."

"It wasn't a moment," Michael said, turning and taking her hands in his. "It wasn't one particular moment. It's a continual thing. It's every time I'm with you, and when I'm not. It's when we're making love and it's when we're fighting. It's waking up in the middle of the night and seeing you there next to me and thinking how lucky I am to be married to you. It's like having a secret you can't wait to tell someone, but then I don't want to tell it because it's just between you and me. God, Jane, it's so corny, it's like bad writing from some idiotic television miniseries, but all the cliches are true. You're my best friend and my partner and my lover. There's no one moment with me and I'm sorry I can't give you one, because I just keep falling in love with you, every day. It just scares me to death to think I could lose you someday and you'd be gone."

Now Jane felt like she was about to cry. She felt as if she were just meeting him for the first time. Maybe that was what he was trying to tell her. She fell into his arms and kissed him, and it was a kiss as good as any they'd ever known. When she was done, she was a slobbering mess, more in love with him than ever.

"Do you have anything else to say to me?" she said.

"Yeah," he told her. "Left-over pasta will be fine."

In Beverly Hills, Kelly was eating left-over pizza when she heard a knock on the front door. Her mother and new stepfather were out for the evening, so she went to answer it. Her heart nearly stopped when she saw it was Jake.

"What are you doing here?" she asked him.

"I don't know," he said. "I just know I had to come." He looked unbelievably handsome in the moonlight. She saw his motorcycle parked in the driveway, and an extra helmet lashed to the seat. She was dressed in jeans and a ratty old sweatshirt, with no makeup on and her hair a mess. All the same, she was so glad to see him she wanted to scream.

"I don't want your money," she said. "I mailed the envelope you left back to you."

"Good," Jake said. "I've only got ten bucks. I didn't come about the money." She looked adorable, standing in the doorway, not dressed up, not made up, just a sweet girl with a good heart. "Sometimes I'm not real good at expressing myself. I guess this is one of those times." He felt a breeze against his neck. In Beverly Hills, even the breezes smelled sweet. "I'm sorry, Kelly. For the way I treated you."

"It's not your fault," she said.

"I just—I don't know what it is between us. And I can't promise anything. But losing your friendship is the wrong way to go. All you've done is try to be my friend, and I don't want to lose that."

"I don't either," she said.

He smiled, his hair falling down across his forehead. "Look, you wanna go for a ride down to the beach?" he asked. "Full moon tonight."

"I have to be home by midnight," she told him.

"Me, too," he said.

* * *

It was just the four of them, Jake, Kelly, Harley and Davidson. On Pico Boulevard, they passed Billy in his cab. He'd been working the swing-shift, mostly because he needed to get Marcy off his mind, and there was nothing like driving the streets of L.A. to get some serious thinking done. Part of your brain was busy steering the cab, and part was busy just reading signs and noticing people and neon lights, and somehow there wasn't enough brain left over to worry too much or persecute yourself with guilt or second thoughts.

When he got home, Alison was standing on a ladder, having nearly finished painting the living room. She looked really cute in her painting overalls, Billy thought, then quickly told himself not to entertain such notions. Cute or not, she was just his roommate, and nothing was going to screw that part of it up. She held out her hands when she saw him, as if to say, well, what do you think? He nodded.

"You wanna help?" she asked.

"Sure," he said.

"Grab a brush," she said, "but watch the drips. I promised Michael we wouldn't get any on the carpeting." She'd spread a heavy plastic drop cloth, but even so, Billy took care not to spill. He began by edging around the window frames.

"It's over," he told her, feeling oddly matter-of-fact about it now. The drive had helped.

"I'm sorry."

"You knew it wouldn't last."

"I didn't know. I think, actually, I was afraid it 1."

"I think I was afraid of the same thing," Billy said. "If I hadn't been on such an ego trip . . ."

"It can make you feel really good to have somebody fall for you like that," Alison said. No one had ever fallen for her like that, but she could imagine it felt good.

"Billy, I want you to know—we can talk, if you want to."

"You mean like friends?" he asked.

"Right," she said. "Like friends."

"Worth a try," he said, returning his attention to his painting. "What a weekend."

"No kidding," Alison said.

They painted until midnight, and then Alison said she had to wash up and get some sleep.

Billy was in bed before Letterman, glad to be alone. He hoped Marcy felt better. Maybe she was already in love with somebody else. He needed to get to sleep because he had a lot of work to do the next day, and he didn't mean driving a cab or teaching dance.

He slept like a baby, only disturbed slightly at three in the morning by the sound of a pipe bursting down in the courtyard, water spurting into the pool like a fountain.

It was the pipe Michael and Jake had thought they'd fixed, but it would wait until the morning.

10

BILLY'S FINGERS DANCED OVER THE COM-
puter keyboard. He licked his lips as he watched the
words appear like magic on the screen.

FADE IN:

INT. A SEEDY JAZZ CLUB
A four-star dive. Smoke hangs in the air like cob-
webs as shadow-shrouded couples gyrate to the
insinuating sax riffs of a sweaty jazz combo. CAM-
ERA SNAKES its way among the dancers, a
bizarro array of upscale sophistos and low-down
hipsters, ZEROING IN ON . . .

A DANGEROUS BLONDE

with whiplash hips in a hot-pink skirt and stiletto heels, doing a sexy navel-scratcher with two captivated boy toys. THE BLONDE'S ice-blue eyes fasten on something across the room.

ANGLE - THE BLONDE'S P.O.V.
as smoke and dancers part like the Red Sea to reveal
. . . BILLY, part Bogart, part Mickey Rourke, all film-noir hunk with five o'clock shadow, Armani duds and attitude to spare.

He threads his way to THE BLONDE, head bobbing to the beat, bedroom eyes fixed half-mast on his prey.

ANGLE—THE BLONDE

With nary a glance, she dusts off her twin hunks, irresistibly drawn to this swaggering stud. BILLY and BLONDE undulate to the music. Eyes locked. Neither daring to blink.

> BILLY
> You're good, kitten. Real good.

> BLONDE
> (almost a purr)
> And when I'm bad . . . I'm just the
> way
> you like it.

BLONDE moves close to BILLY. He curls his lips contemptuously.

> BILLY
So cold, so exciting, so deadly . . .

> BLONDE
So what?

> BILLY
You killed my partner, doll . . . And
now
I'm sending you over.

BLONDE just smiles, grinding her hips against our
steely hero.

> BLONDE
That fish is four days old. I won't
buy it.

BILLY takes out a pair of handcuffs, dangles them
before her.

> BLONDE
You love me too much.
(desperation mounts)
You know you do. You said you do.

> BILLY
If you get life, I'll come and visit
you. If you get the chair . . . I'll
still come and visit you.

With lightning speed, the BLONDE whips a pistol

from her cleavage. BILLY grabs her gun hand. They struggle for ownership, never breaking rhythm with the music. MOVE IN SKIN TIGHT ON BILLY and BLONDE as . . . the gun FIRES once.

By the look on their faces, either of them could have taken the bullet. As they clutch each other tightly, the music fades. As she slumps to the floor, BLONDE hands BILLY her cigarette and then dies.

"Hello . . ." a voice sang out. "Good morning. Ground control to Major Billy."

Billy looked up from his computer screen. It was Alison, ready for work, dressed for success in her pinstripes and power bow. He looked out the window, surprised to see that the sun had come up. He'd worked straight through the night, and barely noticed the passage of time.

"Burning the midnight oil, are we?" she asked.

"Alison," he said, "I am on a roll. A fuel-injected locomotive on a nonstop ride to glory. How many '*t*'s in 'bloodsplattered?'"

"Two," she said. "Weren't you supposed to pick up your cab an hour ago?"

"The hell with my cab, the hell with my dispatcher. A few pages more and I'll get to use the two most excellent words in the English language— 'The End.' When I sell this script, I'll be able to buy the cab company."

"One '*g*' in 'rigor mortis,'" Alison said, reading over his shoulder. "Excuse me, Norman Mailer, but what happened to the Great American Novel?"

"What's wrong with the Great American Screenplay?" he asked. "These things are selling for a million bucks all over town."

"Just as long as you're still able to come up with the rent," she reminded him, then set her coffee cup in the sink.

"Here's looking at you, kid," Billy said, doing what Alison assumed was an imitation of Humphrey Bogart, though it sounded more like Jack Nicholson on Quaaludes. On her way to the car, she passed Jane and Michael, who were skimming the pool.

When Alison was gone, Jane snuck up behind Michael and nibbled on his ear. "Ooh, baby," he said, pausing from his task. "What are you trying to do to me?"

"Just a little taste," she said provocatively. "Tonight we celebrate."

"Celebrate what," he said, turning to her and smiling at the idea.

"Nothing in particular," she said. "I'm going to re-create the first night we spent in L.A. Starting with hot dogs at Pink's . . ."

"Heavy on the chili," he added, glad to have scored a point or two by remembering.

"Then home to watch a video of *Ghost*, followed by candlelight while the stereo plays our song, followed by hours of mad passionate love-making."

"All of this preceded by more hours of mad passionate lovemaking," he said, kissing her and unbuttoning the top button of her sun dress. "Call in sick," he whispered. "Better yet, call in dead—I'm a doctor—I'll sign the certificate." She pulled away from him.

"Get a grip on yourself, Dr. Mancini," she said. "Literally, if you have to. Save it for tonight. It's going to be special."

"It's going to be a long day at the hospital," he reminded her, sorry to inject a note of reality.

"Good things come," she whispered in his ear, "to those who wait."

In his other ear, Michael heard a clanking sound coming from the laundry room, meaning one of the washing machines was out of balance on the spin cycle.

The sound stopped when Sandy redistributed the load. Across the room, Jake was examining a bed sheet which had a blue stain on it that resembled Rhode Island.

"First rule of living alone," Sandy advised. "Never mix your blues and your whites."

"You're an expert on the blues now?"

"I am."

"I live alone and like it," Jake said.

"You live alone and look it," Sandy told him, helping him fold his sheets. "Expecting company tonight?"

"Why do you ask?"

"Come on Jake," she said. "The only time you wash your sheets is when you're having somebody over, and I do mean having somebody. Who is it this time? Slumber party with your little Beverly Hills princess, what was her name . . . Chloe?"

"Kelly," Jake informed her, fishing in his pockets for change.

"My, my," Sandy said. "I never have seen you so serious about somebody, after all of what, three dates? Four? So tell me Jake, is it the girl or the money?" Jake glared at her. He wanted to tell her it wasn't the money, but, unfortunately, just at that moment he needed to borrow a quarter. She loaned it to him with a knowing smile. "You know what they say where I come from, Jake? The best traps have the sweetest bait."

"She's not trying to trap me," Jake said. "She's a friend. The problem is, she wants to be more. Like my life isn't screwed up enough already." Sandy helped him fold another sheet. "Nothing's happened. Nothing's gonna happen."

"And Kelly," Sandy said. "Is she aware of this?"

"No," Jake admitted. "Not yet, anyway. She's coming over for dinner tonight and I'm just going to lay it out for her."

Sandy smiled, thinking, sure Jake, but wash your sheets, just in case.

"It's not going to be easy," Jake continued, "this girl just doesn't know when to quit."

"You'll find a way, Jake. You always do."

"I just don't want to hurt her."

"Better quick and painful than slow and agonizing," Sandy recommended. "Believe me, I know." She picked her laundry basket up off the dryer, leaving Jake to deal with the rest of his dirty laundry alone.

Kelly was preparing for her date by doing what she did best, which was shopping. Ordinarily Rodeo Drive would have been her street of preference, but for a funkier, more up-to-date look—the kind Jake would be more likely to respond to—she decided to try some of the boutiques on Melrose, and she'd brought Steve and David with her to give her their masculine opinions.

"On the one hand," Kelly was saying, rifling through a rack at a place called simply Très, "I could go with a tie-around blouse with lots of bare midriff, but I don't want to come off too obvious."

"Besides, your belly's too white," Steve submitted.

"Then again, a gray ribbed tank-top would do fine, but then I couldn't wear a bra," she continued.

"Whatever happened to playing hard to get?" her stepbrother David asked.

"Not tonight," Kelly said. "Tonight nobody is playing." She didn't mean to sound like a condescending snob, but that was simply how she felt about it. No more high school games or juvenile antics. Tonight was grown-up stuff, real world, raw emotions and serious moonlight. Needless to say, Steve and David kept trying to tell her what a fall she was headed for. David even suggested Jake was manipulating Kelly, playing the tragic hardcase and appealing to her mothering instincts.

"You don't understand," she told him. "Jake's just going through a hard time."

"So's the guy he hit at the unemployment agency," Steve said, as they circled a display of polo shirts.

"He didn't hit anybody," she said. "Look, he needs me on his side, to be there for him."

"Kelly, I think he gets the idea. You call him five times a day," David argued. "Of course, he never calls back."

"David, just shut up," she snapped. This was not the kind of advice she'd brought them along for.

"Kelly," Steve said. "Believe it or not, we care about you."

"Thank you for your concern," she replied. "I think I know what I'm doing."

At D&D Advertising, it was business as usual, which, for Alison, meant saying one of four things, "D&D Advertising, may I help you?" "One moment and I'll check," "He's in a meeting at the moment," or, "He's on another line. Can I have him call you back?" It was a job for a parrot. She was transferring a call from a fax machine to a computer—they were probably getting together to discuss how machines were going to take over the world—she wished them luck—when a package landed on her desk with a thunderous boom.

"Special delivery," Billy said. Alison quickly surmised that the package was a screenplay. She opened the cover and read the title page.

"*The Big Shock?*"

"Catchy title, eh?" Billy cooed. "I can see the ads now, '*The Big Shock* is the Big Shock.'"

She lifted the manuscript to estimate the weight. "Congratulations," she told him. "It seems heavy enough."

"One hundred twenty pages of blood, sweat and tears, hot off the Xerox machine," he said anxiously. "For your eyes only."

"Why, Billy," she said, trying to sound enthusiastic. "You mean I'm the first person you're giving it to? I don't know what to say . . ."

"Just read it," he said. "Tomorrow I'm dropping it off with every agent in town, so I need some constructive criticism by tonight. Be brutally honest, no punches pulled. And guard it with your life—we don't want a million-dollar script falling into the wrong hands."

"We certainly don't," she said. "I'm really swamped here but . . . I'll see what I can do."

"Thanks," he said, clenching both fists in apparent victory. "I feel like a real writer now. It feels great."

At Couture, where Jane worked, three club bunnies with big hair were searching the racks for clothes to wear to trap and seduce, and in general win the hearts and minds of men, not to mention the rest of their anatomy. One held up an armored bustier with chain-mail cups.

"Lethal, definitely lethal," her friend said.

"It'd be a waste to wear it to Boom Town," a second said. "That club is at least six months old."

"We can do the rave party at Dee-Lite," the third said. "That rad deejay should be working."

"The one with the beehive pompadour? I'll take the buff stallion behind the bar at Orbit over him any time."

"So we start at Boom Town, go to Orbit and end up at Dee-Lite. Or else we start at Dee-Lite, go to Orbit and end up at Boom Town."

"Dear me! So many choices, so little time . . ."

Jane kept her eye on them to make sure they weren't shoplifting, though from the looks of them they didn't seem the type, just innocent, sweet girls, not that much younger than Jane, out to have a frantic good time, enjoying the thrill of the chase. The way Jane used to.

She crossed over to Rhonda, who'd come in to return the dress she'd borrowed for her "date" with Daniel. The three girls giggled loudly over some private joke.

"Sometimes I forget how much fun it is, being single," Jane said.

Rhonda was trying on earrings. "If you want to trade places with me, just let me know," Rhonda said.

"I liked club hopping," Jane said. "I was good at it. I liked walking into a place thinking, you know, wow, anything could happen to me tonight. There was just so much possibility."

"Be thankful you're not like them," Rhonda

said. "You think they wouldn't trade a lifetime pass at the Roxbury to be married and in love, with someone always waiting for you at home?"

Jane thought of the time she and Michael had almost gone to the Roxbury, but then he'd gotten a migraine. Sometimes lately, when she found herself at a party or club alone, she wasn't sure what the hell she was doing there. Such places are arenas, where the mating game is played. She was on the bench now, like a retired quarterback calling plays from his rocking chair.

"The grass always looks greener on the other side of the fence," Rhonda was saying, "until you see the weeds."

The phone rang. Jane answered it and smiled when she heard Michael's voice. Jane was surprised at the coincidence and told him she'd just been thinking about him.

"Look, Jane," he said, "about tonight . . ." She steeled herself, knowing exactly what was coming next. "I'm stuck on call again. Nelman wants me to assist a coronary by-pass. Remember that crabby old patient, the one who cursed me in Italian? I'm getting odds when we open him up we don't even find a heart. I'll try to be home by midnight, so I was thinking I'll bring some hot dogs and then we can watch *Ghost* until we cry like babies."

"I'm the one who cries," she reminded him in a cool voice. "You never cry."

"I love you," Michael said, as if that was supposed to make everything better. Sometimes it did, but tonight it didn't. She told him she loved him, too, because that was what she always said.

When she got home after work, to her empty apartment, she made a quick dinner of Kraft Macaroni and Cheese, accompanied by a piece of raisin toast, and washed down with a glass of iced tea. She felt guilty for taking in unnecessary calories, but she could understand why some women got fat after they got married. Staying thin didn't seem nearly as imperative. She decided to swim laps in the pool to work the calories off, and had just completed her thirtieth when she saw Sandy, in a dress that made Dolly Parton look like the queen of subtlety.

"Watcha doin'?" Sandy teased. "Getting in shape for your special night with Doctor Stud-Muffins?"

"It's off," Jane said, contemplating another thirty laps. "They need him at the hospital."

"You mean I soundproofed my walls for nothing?" Sandy said. Jane gave up on swimming and climbed out of the pool. Sandy handed her a towel.

"It was just a silly excuse to celebrate anyway," Jane said, drying her face.

"You know what you need Jane?" Sandy said. "You need a night at Shooters. Get yourself good and toasted. Friday nights are always jumping. Rhonda'll be there, you can help her forage for beefcake."

"Sandy, please," Jane said. "Thanks all the same, but I'll wait up for Michael."

"You're always waiting up for Michael," Sandy taunted. "You're on call more than he is. Who do you think you are, Mrs. Marcus Welby?"

"Marcus Welby was a widower," Jane said.

"And what are you?" Sandy replied. "For God's sakes, you're 23 years old. Life is passing you by— have some fun. Be independent for a change. See if you can enjoy yourself without your husband. Prove you're not a prisoner of that wedding band. I dare you."

"What is this, the third grade?" Jane responded, trying not to show that deep down, part of her probably agreed with Sandy. "Look, I love my husband, I love my life, everything is roses and sunshine, so go to work, would you?"

"Suit yourself," Sandy said, walking away. Then she paused and said, over her shoulder, "I double dog dare you."

Jane laughed, but when Sandy was gone, Jane stopped laughing. Maybe part of the problem was that, when you're single, like Sandy, love seems a rare thing, and every night you find it seems like a victory, your efforts paying off in a concrete tangible way. When you're married, love is a constant, and no particular night seems like a victory, and you don't know how to measure your progress. Maybe you don't feel like you're making progress at all. It was strange, she thought, because even though it's hard work, sometimes you still feel like you've stopped trying. She didn't want to ever stop trying.

Michael was in the on-call room, playing cards with the other interns and discussing their various patients, when they heard a knock at the door. Usually nobody knocked on the door, since it was a place where anybody on staff could rest or catch up on their sleep, and in general come and go at will. When he opened the door, he saw his wife. Jane was wearing a daring backless black dress with a peek-a-boo neckline, hose and heels, heavy on the makeup, as sexy as she could make herself on relatively short notice. In her hands she held a tray on which was a platter of Pink's hot dogs, heavy on the chili, surrounded by three candles. And in her purse she had a cassette player playing the song she and Michael considered their song, a tune called, appropriately enough, "Don't Wait That Long". Michael looked both pleased and a little embarrassed.

"Guys," he said to the three other interns in the room. "This is my wife. Jane, these are . . . the guys."

"Hi," Jane said to them. Waiting. Being doctors, they were smart enough to take the hint, and got up to give Jane and Michael some privacy, one of them saying, "Let's go, there's gotta be somebody sick in this place." Michael was moved beyond words. He turned off the lights and cleared a pile of medical journals from the table, where Jane set the platter down.

"One candle for each month we've lived in L.A.," she said, smiling at him. Trying.

"I don't . . . I don't know what to say," he said. He leaned across the table and kissed her gently.

"Don't say anything," Jane said, putting a finger

to his lips. "It's a special night no matter where we celebrate it." He pushed the platter aside and kissed her again. She moved closer to him and shivered as he ran his fingertips down her bare back. When she heard Michael's beeper go off, she pretended for as long as she could that it was a bird chirping, a nightingale perhaps. They'd been interrupted so many times before that Michael didn't have to say anything. He went to the phone. Jane gathered from eavesdropping that he had to report to pre-op' to get ready for the by-pass operation. Such things were important, and she tried hard to conceal her disappointment. He kissed her quickly and made for the door, waiting for her there. She smiled.

"Honey," he told her, "why don't you get out of the house tonight? Go be with your friends and have some fun." Jane noted the irony, Michael saying the same thing Sandy had said. She kissed Michael good-bye, telling him she wasn't sure what she was going to do, but when she got back to Melrose Place, she knew she couldn't bear to go in to her empty apartment again.

Shooters was jamming, wall to wall with movers and shakers, models and actors, the quick and the dead, the good and the bad—the ugly seemed to have stayed home. Rhonda and Jane sat at the bar, where Jane nursed a glass of white wine. She'd decided maybe people were right, maybe she'd been hanging on too tightly lately, and it was time to let her hair down a little. Within reason. Rhonda was scoping out the available men the way a shark surveys a school of squid, voraciously and without excessive selectivity.

"Is it my imagination," Jane asked, "or have guys gotten better looking? I've been out of circulation too long."

"You just have a better view without Michael here," Rhonda said, sipping her drink through a straw. "Don't worry Janie, I'll protect you from the big bad wolves."

At that moment, Jane and Rhonda simultaneously noticed two unquestionably hot-looking guys staring at them from the other side of the pool tables. Jane could admit to herself that they were hot-looking, merely an empirical observation, the way one might regard a painting—there was nothing personal about it.

"Oh my," Rhonda giggled. "And they are looking right at us, aren't they?"

Jane looked away.

"Bullseye, Jane," a voice from behind the bar said. "You've bagged yourself a prize." Jane turned to see Sandy standing at the tap, drawing a beer. "Of course, a serious predator has to kill and eat her prey if she wants to maintain her place in the food chain."

"Thanks anyway, Sandy, but I had chili dogs for dinner."

"Leave Janie alone, girlfriend," Rhonda said. "She's just here to take notes." Jane looked again in the direction of the two guys who'd been observing them. Without meaning to, or did she mean to, she locked eyes with one of them.

"You know what they say," she told Sandy and Rhonda. "Just because you've ordered dinner doesn't mean you can't still read what's on the menu."

"Face it, Jane," Sandy said, "you're here for one reason and one reason only. You want to find out if you still got it. But I guess you'll never know, as long as you're wearing that cute little wedding band." Sandy wandered down the bar to wait on a customer. Jane watched her, wondering if what Sandy said was true. Was Jane really *only* wondering if she could still attract a stranger? Still turn a head and feel that ego rush she'd always felt when she knew somebody was coming on to her, that sense of danger and excitement?

"Don't look now," Rhonda said sotto voce. "Hunk attack at twelve o'clock high." In the mirror behind the bar, Jane saw that the two men who'd been staring at them were headed their way. In a moment's impulse, she slid the wedding band from her finger and slipped it into the pocket of her black silk jacket.

11

KELLY AND JAKE WERE SHOPPING FOR groceries at a Safeway three blocks down from Shooters, strolling up and down the aisles, planning the dinner they were going to have together. Kelly had never had a man cook dinner for her before, but it seemed perfectly romantic to her, the perfect beginning to a night she hoped would be, finally, everything she'd been dreaming about. Dreaming was one of her best skills. Her only worry was that somewhere down the line, she'd have to reciprocate, because cooking was one of her worst skills. Her best dish, okay, her only dish, was beanie-wienie casserole, but then, Jake didn't seem like the kind of guy who needed to be impressed with fancy food. Right now, it was romantic enough, just cruising the ice cream section.

"Chocolate Chip Cookie Dough," she said, picking up a gallon. "My absolute favorite. Jake, this is so much better than eating out. Just the two of us, spending a quiet night at your place, making it. The lasagna, I mean." He didn't seem to catch her naughty joke, but at the checkout counter, she got a second chance to drop him a hint, a special display of imported cheeses. She picked up a wedge and showed it to him as he began to empty their cart onto the conveyor belt.

"Reggiano Parmesan," she said, handing it to him. "It's said to be a potent aphrodisiac." He looked cautiously at the price.

"Six bucks," he said. "What a turn-on."

"Come on Jake, my treat," she said, meaning only that she wanted to help out with the cost of the meal. Quickly she realized she'd hurt his pride, implying that he needed her help to pay for things.

"Don't worry about it," he said, throwing it on the conveyor belt with the rest of their purchases.

"I'm sorry Jake," she said. "I know things are tough for you right now."

"You don't know the half of it," he said with a weak smile.

"I just want to make everything perfect, you know?" she told him, taking his hand in hers. "I want to make everything right."

Jake stared at her, as if he was trying to apologize for something. She smiled to tell him there was nothing to apologize for. The checkout girl told them the total came to forty-four dollars and twenty cents.

When Jake opened his wallet, Kelly saw that he only had two twenties. She pretended she hadn't noticed and quickly grabbed the gallon of Chocolate Chip Cookie Dough ice cream.

"I changed my mind," she said. "Too much cholesterol. I'll just take this back." She hoped she'd acted in time to prevent Jake from losing face in front of the checkout girl. She was really beginning to understand him, and she knew such things were important to him. When she looked over her shoulder, the look on his face told her he was finally beginning to appreciate her. It was a very good sign.

Alison doubted very much that Billy was going to appreciate her. When she arrived home after work, she found Matt Fielding locking his apartment door, getting ready to go out for a night on the town from the looks of him. At least one of the men living at Melrose Place had a sense of style. He also always had an ear he was willing to lend, and when he saw Alison, he was perceptive enough to note she looked like Susan Hayward at the end of *I Want to Live*, marching toward the gas chamber.

"Evening Alison," he greeted her. "Marathon day at the office, huh?"

"Understatement of the year," she admitted. She held up Billy's manuscript. "Stayed late to do some reading."

"Well, hey," he said cheerfully. "An artist friend of mine is throwing a party out in Laurel Canyon. You should come with me. I guarantee it'll be wild."

"I've had enough excitement for one day, thanks," she told him. "I read Billy's script."

"No fooling," Matt said diplomatically. "Billy wrote a script?"

"He certainly did," Alison said, shifting the ream of paper nervously from hand to hand.

"I take it it's not a comedy."

"Not intentionally," she said, taking a seat on a nearby bench. Matt sat down next to her. "Matt, it's awful. It's worse than awful. It's a mishmash of every bad movie that was ever made. And the worst of it is, Billy thinks it's great. He thinks he's going to sell it for a million dollars. All his dreams are riding on this." She crashed her head on Matt's shoulder in anguish that was not entirely mocked. "What am I going to tell him?"

"You could lie to spare his feelings," Matt suggested. "Although that would encourage false hopes."

"If I nuke him with what I really think, he'll be devastated," she said. "He'll be home in a little while, and I don't want to face him. Matt, how can I?"

"Alison," Matt said. "You can't hide forever. After all, he uses the same bathroom as you. Sooner or later you know what you're going to have to do."

"Shoot myself?"

"Make him a nice dinner first," Matt said as an afterthought. "It'll soften the blow." Alison couldn't think of any dish she knew how to make that would do the trick.

At Shooters, Delia Saldana was playing hostess to a friendly group gathered at the end of the bar, a four-some comprised of Rhonda, Jane, and two men who had joined them. The one with long hair was named

Peter. The other one seemed to be paying more attention to Rhonda. His name was Alex, and he was shier than Peter, with Latino features and a warm smile.

Jane, fully intending to keep things under control, had ordered a Virgin Mary. Peter offered to pay for it.

"No really," Jane said, digging in her pocketbook. "I'd like to pay." Peter, however, had a five-dollar bill in his hand and handed it to Delia, who made some crack about "desire one, purity zero." Rhonda picked up the small talk where it had left off when the drinks arrived. Peter was definitely focusing all of his attention on Jane. She couldn't deny it. She liked it.

"So you guys are in a rock and roll band?" Rhonda asked. "Do we know you? Should we know you?"

"Well, uh, the fact is, at present—" Alex began.

"Actually we just formed the group," Peter interrupted. "No agent, no record deal, no following. But we've got songs and we do own our own instruments."

"Well," Rhonda said. "Even Guns 'n' Roses had their hungry years. I was going to say lean years, but you can't get much leaner than Axl Rose."

"Or meaner," Jane added.

"Aspiring rock stars, you can buy by the pound in this town," Peter said to Jane. "Your story has got to be more exciting than ours."

"Not very," she said. "I work in a boutique on Melrose."

"Well, that figures," he said. "You've got style to spare. I'm serious! Look at you—it's like you're lit from within by a piece of the sun." Jane had heard corny awful pick-up lines in her time, but never one as fabulously corny and awful as that.

"Pete writes the lyrics in the band," Alex said.

"Careful, Peter," Rhonda warned him. "There's a speed limit in this state."

"So I get a ticket." He shrugged. "I'll throw myself on the mercy of the court. But seriously, Jane, someone as incredible looking as you has got to have a boyfriend." Jane and Rhonda exchanged furtive glances, Rhonda waiting for Jane to decide how to respond.

"Technically speaking?" Jane said. "No, I don't have a boyfriend." If I can't stand the heat, Jane thought, I can always get out of the kitchen.

In her own kitchen, Alison felt the heat increasing. She was pulling a tuna casserole out of the oven when Billy walked in the door, still excited about his script, she gathered from his greeting.

"L-u-u-cy, I'm home," he called out as he slammed the door behind him.

"In the kitchen, Ricky," she answered him.

Billy strode in, bouncing off the walls. "Man, what a day," he said. "One hard case after the other. 'Driver, you're going too slow. Driver, you're going too fast, you're missing the lights, isn't there a shortcut?' I'm telling you, when I sell my script, we're going to have an I-quit-my-job party the likes of which this place has never seen."

"Well, I hope you worked up an appetite," she

said smoothly. "I'm making tuna casserole for two."

"Really?" he said. "I love tuna casserole."

"I know," Alison said. "You told me." Billy looked astonished.

"You made me dinner." he said suspiciously. "What's the catch?"

"There's no catch," Alison lied. "I just whipped this up from stuff I found in the refrigerator. It's no big deal."

"No big deal?" he said. "From the person who was going to call in the SWAT team just because I asked for a spoonful of peanut butter? Alison, this can only mean one thing—you finished my script." Alison could only nod. "And this is your way of congratulating me, right? Of telling me you loved it."

"Billy," Alison said, wishing she were dead. "It was just that I thought—"

"Thank you, Lord, thank you! I knew I could trust her judgment," Billy said, dancing around the kitchen in steps Alison didn't think he'd learned at Arthur Murray. "After all, you were an English major. I mean, what better validation could I hope for? I gotta admit, there were times there when I didn't think I'd finish. You know how it is, you get afraid you won't measure up, so you avoid the question by not finishing things and making excuses. But I guess every writer goes through things like that. All it takes is believing in yourself." He paused a moment. Alison was frozen, tongue-tied. "But here I am, gassing away and not giving you a chance to get a word in edgewise. So?" he asked. Then the two words Alison had been dreading. "Whudya think?"

"Oh my God, Billy," she said. "I think the pasta is boiling over." She made a fast break for the stove.

Jane had not played pinball in years, but was at that moment doing a good impersonation of the Pinball Wizardess, tapping the flippers like a pro and using body English like Joe Cocker with ants in his shorts. Rhonda, Alex, and Peter were cheering her on.

"Do it, girlfriend," Rhonda said, squeezing Alex's arm excitedly. "Rack 'em up."

"Easy, Rhonda," Alex said good-naturedly, pulling his arm free. "That's one of the arms I use to play bass with."

"Sorry," Rhonda said, batting her eyelashes at him. "I'm just passionate by nature." Jane gave the machine one nudge too hard, making the tilt light light up and an electronic voice from inside the machine boom out "YOU LOSE, SUCKER!" The game went dark. All four of them groaned loudly

"Lost my touch," Jane said. "I was the pinball princess of Lake Bluff High School."

"Okay, Lady Jane," Peter said, laying another quarter down on the glass. "One more time for your alma mater." Jane looked at her watch.

"Look," she said, "it was great meeting you, Peter, but I really think I should be heading home."

"You can't be serious," Peter said as Jane slipped her jacket back on. "It's early. There are third graders still up. Look, Alex and I had made plans to cut out soon anyway. There's a totally happening club downtown, real secret and exclusive, one of those possibly illegal after-hours joints, but it's open now."

"The bouncer plays drums in our band," Alex added. "Otherwise we wouldn't even know about it."

"You guys gotta come," Peter insisted.

"You can tell me about it tomorrow," Jane said, begging off, even though she'd always wanted to see one of those after-hour clubs that would open for a week in one location, then move on, one step ahead of the liquor commission. Rhonda asked the guys to excuse her a second and took Jane aside, speaking in urgent if hushed tones.

"Janie, come with us, please, please, please . . ." she begged.

"Rhonda," Jane said, "whatever happened to all the stuff you were saying about the grass being greener on the other side of the fence?"

"That was before I met Alex," Rhonda said. "Look Jane, there might be a chance with this guy, but I can't go to this place with him alone, I need back up. Peter's a nice enough guy, isn't he? It's not like it would kill you."

"He also thinks I'm single," Jane reminded her friend.

"So, keep it casual," Rhonda said. "You can manage it."

Jane considered. She didn't want to let her friend down. And it was hardly ten o'clock yet, early by anybody's standards. In her prime, she wouldn't have stopped partying until the sky was light enough to make the streetlights blink off. She made Rhonda promise her she'd be home by midnight.

Billy was pounding down his second helping of
tuna casserole, having explained that he'd been too
excited to stop for lunch. He wanted to talk about
his script. All Alison had managed to do so far was
ask a few questions to clarify things, and give non-
committal responses to Billy's questions.

"How about the part where the hero swan dives
off the balcony and blows away three bad guys
before landing in the pool," Billy wanted to know.
"Pretty outrageous, eh?"

"Totally," Alison nodded, then averted her eyes.
She picked up a few dirty dishes and took them into
the kitchen.

"And the ending?" he called after her. "Did it
catch you by surprise?"

"You mean where the killer turned out to be a
transsexual ex-nun?" she answered back, trying to
keep a straight face. "Absolutely."

She returned to the dining table, resolved to
bring on the moment of truth. Honesty was the best
policy. At least when purchasing a one-way ticket to
Pago Pago was out of the question.

"So come on, Alison," Billy said. "What do you
think? Is it really good enough?"

She sighed. "The truth?" she asked.

"Absolutely."

"I hated it."

"You're joking. You're not joking."

She shook her head.

He gulped, trying to contain himself. "Okay. What did you hate about it?"

"Everything."

Billy just stared at her. His face was turning bright red. "Would you mind being more specific, please."

"Billy, the story made no sense," she said. For all the practicing she done, waiting for him to get home, she still wasn't sure how to put it. "The characters weren't even real."

He pushed his plate away and leapt to his feet. "Well dammit, I should've never given it to you," he shouted. "What do you know about anything?"

"You're right," Alison said. "You should get a second opinion. I know you have talent—"

"Why'd you make me dinner, to fatten me up for the kill? The trouble with you is, you have no taste. Which is something I wish I could say about your casserole."

"Then don't eat it," Alison said, getting angry herself. She was never good when people started yelling at each other, and she hated how it made her feel.

"Maybe you're just jealous."

"Jealous?"

"As in, green with envy," Billy spat. "Maybe you can't stand seeing me succeed."

"Or maybe you can't take criticism," she countered hotly.

"Not when it's useless," he said. He picked up his coat and stormed out the door. In other words, things had gone roughly the way Alison had expected they would.

*   *   *

Things were going roughly the way Jane had expected them to go as well. The club was in a warehouse, a large brick building with no outward signs that anything was going on inside, except for the line a hundred people long, waiting to get in. She'd hate to see what it would have been like if it hadn't been, as Peter had said, secret and exclusive. They had walked right past the line when the bouncer, the drummer in the band, beckoned them to skip ahead of the others. As they entered the club, Jane couldn't help feeling, well—cool. Just like it used to feel, privileged and free. Nor did she mind walking past all those women with Peter at her side, even if it was only pretend.

Inside, strobe lights flashed as the room throbbed to music so loud it was probably making her ancestors cover their ears. The dance floor felt like one enormous sub-woofer. The crowd was young, sweaty and half-naked, people dancing with delirious abandon. They managed to find a table in the corner, where Peter slid in next to Jane. He'd been talking to her as if there was already something developing between them, and Jane hated herself for being unable to think of a way to tell him he was on the wrong track. Maybe she didn't want to tell him. She wondered.

"Time is tight," he was saying, shouting above the music. "It works against you. It goes slow when you're where you don't belong and fast when you're comfortable. Are you comfortable, Jane?"

"What?" she said. "I can hardly hear you." The music was reaching a crescendo.

"I said 'I want to make mad passionate love to

you,' " he shouted.

This time she understood him perfectly.

"I'm sorry," she shouted. "I still didn't hear you."

"Would you like to dance?" he asked.

"Not really," she said, though she knew it wasn't the truth.

"Aw, come on Jane. Just one song," he pleaded. "Just to wake up our feet. Mine are falling asleep." He smiled again, a charming smile. "What, am I so devastatingly attractive to you that the mere thought of dancing with me turns you to jelly? I don't think so."

She laughed. She wanted to look at her watch again, but decided not to. "Oh, why not?" she said. "What's one dance going to hurt?"

The dance floor was crowded, the music fast and loud, one of those hour-long grooves seamlessly edited to prevent people from saying to themselves "one more and then we'll quit." Then, to Jane's dismay, as soon as she stepped onto the floor, the music changed. It was a song she recognized, the one she'd had playing in her cassette player earlier that night. "Don't Wait That Long." It was her and Michael's song. Peter put his arms around her's and pulled her close, swaying to the music. He was a good dancer, but Jane was not enjoying herself.

12

JAKE HAD A TEAR ROLLING DOWN HIS cheek. He was chopping onions, sweet Vidalia, to go with the arugula and endive and raddichio Kelly had bought for the salad. She knew salads. When Jake made salads, which wasn't often, they tended to consist of lettuce and lettuce, with lettuce on top and then more lettuce. When Kelly finished rinsing the exotic greens, she approached Jake from behind and started nibbling at his neck.

"Kelly," he said, wriggling away from her, "you're not helping the situation here. I've got a sharp knife in my hand."

"It's one way to work up an appetite," she whispered in his ear. "I want to make sure you're still hungry when it's time for dessert." She turned him around. "Oh, you're crying," she teased, "here, let me make it better. I can, you know." She kissed his eyes, his wet cheeks. She couldn't remember a time when she'd felt more sure of herself and of her sexuality. He kissed her back, his excitement growing, she could tell, until he pushed her away. She admired him for his restraint, actually, and if nobody else thought of him as having gentlemanly characteristics, she did. At the same time, when she saw him mustering his willpower, it turned her on and made her feel strong.

"Let's not start anything we can't finish," he said.

"It already started, Jake," she told him. "The moment we met." She kissed him again. "I know you felt something." And again. "And I know what I felt." And again. "And I think it's time we started feeling things together." One more big one ought to do the trick, she thought.

One more big one and he'd be past the point of no return, Jake knew, so he brought the kiss up short, thinking he'd check on the lasagna. But at the last moment, he felt there was something unfinished about the kiss, so he dove back into it, taking Kelly in his arms and holding her close. There was something truly remarkable in the way she responded to his touch, giving to him, softening, following his leads or anticipating them. He felt like a magician, able to change the scenery with a wave of his hand. The temptation was unbearable, but until he thought of what to do about it, he decided he would just keep kissing her. Only the ringing of the telephone, and then the sound of his own recorded voice message playing back from the answering machine, brought him to his senses.

"I'd better get that," he apologized. "It could be work."

"Let the machine answer it," Kelly urged him. "That's why they invented them."

He pulled away from her and picked up the receiver. A familiar voice greeted him, then explained that the caller needed to reschedule an appointment for a half hour later than arranged. Jake said that would be fine, speaking furtively so that Kelly wouldn't hear him. When he hung up, he saw Kelly waiting for him in the kitchen, looking as inviting as a dark, cool spring-fed pond after a 115-degree day spent in the sun. The urge to take the plunge was nearly irresistible.

Jane's resolve was strengthening. Dancing with Peter had been hard enough, but slow dancing with him to the song she and Michael cherished as their own had taken it one step too far. She'd backed off from him, and had almost made it back to the table when a fast tune started. Peter was a good dancer, and was doing his best to get her to have a good time, practically begging her to join him.

"I think I've had enough," she apologized. "I'm just going to sit down."

"Spouse, sister, angel, pilot of fate, whose course has been so starless? Oh, too late, beloved, oh, too soon adorned by me," he sang, acting out the words with broad parodying dramatic gestures, clutching his hands to his heart.

"Percy Bysshe Shelley," Jane said.

"I steal from him in my songs," Peter said. "Helluva poet. Feminist, too. The man worshiped women."

"Including two wives, one of whom committed suicide, a stepsister and a mistress on the side," Jane said, smiling. "I minored in Romantic Lit."

"It shows," Peter said. "You've got class. I mean that in the absolutely best way." He put his arms around her and tried to kiss her, but when he did, Jane managed to pull her head back.

"Don't," she said.

He forced a weak smile. "Looks like I finally got that speeding ticket," he said.

Jane was angry, more at herself than at him. She returned to the table. Peter joined her there. As the music grew quiet again. Jane felt like a jerk. Peter touched her hand. "What's the matter, Jane? Don't you like me?"

"I like you fine, Peter, really . . ."

"Then what's the problem?"

"The problem is," she said, looking him square in the eye, "I'm married."

He stared at her in disbelief.

"Look, if you don't want to hang out with me, just say so. I can take it. I'm a big boy."

"No, I mean it," she said. "It's true."

"Funny," he said, pointing to her left hand. "I don't see a ring."

If that was what it was going to take to convince him, Jane thought, so be it. She picked up her jacket and fished in the pocket for her wedding ring. Not finding it, she searched the other pocket. She turned it inside out. It was empty. She turned the first pocket inside out. It was also empty. A horrible empty feeling grew in the pit of her stomach, and the room suddenly seemed to spin.

"Oh my God," was all she could say, her face drained of color. The ring was gone.

At Shooters, Billy was trying to drown his sorrows, well into his third diet Dr Pepper. He knew that a real writer would probably be saturating himself with tequila or straight bourbon and growling to the help and picking fights with total strangers, but Billy didn't like drinking to excess and, anyway, he didn't feel much like a real writer.

When he looked up into the mirror behind the bar, he saw Alison standing behind him. He didn't say hello, but instead picked up the second half of his Mounds bar. "It's a known fact that sugar is an important source of carbohydrates, which are the body's most important energy source," he said matter-of-factly to his roommate. "Some doctors even think in the form of chocolate, it can cure cancer and put the arms back on the *Venus de Milo*." Alison sat on the stool next to him, trying to make him feel better. Some masochistic part of him forced him to ask, one last time. "Was it really that bad?"

She tried to smile. "Maybe I'm wrong—"

"Just tell me the truth," he interrupted. "It was, wasn't it?"

"I had to be honest, Billy. I wouldn't be able to face you, otherwise."

He threw his unfinished candy bar toward the wastebasket behind the bar. It bounced off a glass cabinet and fell to the floor.

"You know, I've been writing ever since I was a kid," he said, not angry any more, staring at the display of liquor bottles, not wanting to look anybody in the eye just yet, himself included. "Short stories, epic poems, a novel or two. All of them just lying around, waiting to be finished. And here I was, so proud of myself for accomplishing the impossible. I finally completed something. Only now I have to face the million-dollar question. What if I've been lying to myself? All these years, what if I suck? What if I really don't have it?" He downed the rest of his soda as if it was Red Eye just before the shoot-out at the OK Corral. "My dad would love that, boy. He's been trying to get me to work at his furniture store for years. He thinks writing is a hobby, not a profession. Something women do during summer vacation." He stared at his ice. "What if my dad is right?"

"Nobody said it was going to be easy, Billy," Alison told him, putting a hand on his shoulder. "This is just your first shot. Sometimes it takes a while to get to where you want to be. William Kennedy didn't get famous for *Ironweed* until he was well into his fifties. In the meantime, you're going to have to learn to deal with rejection and failure, and figure out how to accept it and just go on with things."

"Just go on," Billy said. "Simple as that."

"All it takes is believing in yourself," she said. "Those were your own words, remember?"

"Yeah, well," he said. "What do I know?"

There was nothing more that Alison could say, and perhaps nothing more Billy wanted to hear, so she left him where he sat. She didn't know what she would do the next time he gave her something to read. But, judging from the way he was feeling, there wasn't going to be a next time. There might not even be anything more to read.

Jane had gotten down on her knees to look under the table. Rhonda was with her, while Peter and Alex were looking behind the cushions in the booth.

"You're absolutely certain you had it when we came in here?" Rhonda asked.

"I know I did, I'm sure I did," Jane said.

"What the hey?" Alex offered. "You can always get another one."

"From where?" Jane said, not meaning to snap at him. "Sicily? Sicily a hundred and fifty years ago? The ring was an heirloom. It belonged to my husband's great-grandmother."

"Alex and I'll talk to the bouncer," Rhonda said quickly. "Maybe he knows if somebody turned it in."

Jane crawled over to the neighboring booth, the love struck couple seated there ignoring her prying hands between their feet.

"It's getting close to midnight," Peter said. "Are you sure your car won't turn back into a pumpkin?" She ignored him, though she didn't blame him for being mad at her. He got down on his knees next to her to help her look. "Why'd you do it, Jane? Why the charade in the first place?"

"Look," Jane said, beginning to give up hope of finding her ring, "you asked me if I had a boyfriend and I told you the truth. I don't."

"Is married life really such a drag?" he asked.

"It's wonderful, dammit," she said grabbing at an object on the dirty floor.

"Then why'd you lead me on?"

"Because I'm stupid, that's why," she said dropping the tab from a beer can. "Because things don't always go your way, so you listen to people who are lonely and scared and jealous of everything they don't have, who . . . I was going to say who have it in for you, but that's not true. I did it because you forget. You know yourself, your whole life, as one person, and then you change into a different person, and it feels frightening and unfamiliar, so you think for a night you can go back, just to get your bearings, so you think—" Suddenly her heart raced. Underneath the seat of a booth two tables over, tucked into a crevice, she saw something glisten. When she got there, she had to pick up a man's foot to clear the way, reaching desperately for the shiny object, only to find it was . . . a piece of ice.

"Did you lose something?" the man asked her as he peered down at Jane.

"Everything," Jane replied.

After supper was over, Jake had gone into the kitchen to clean up the dishes. Ordinarily he had enough clean dishes to last him a week or two between washings, having learned, as most bachelors do, to conserve effort by often eating directly from the pan. Tonight, he did the dishes because he needed to stall for time. Every minute that Kelly was there, his resolve weakened. To make matters worse, they'd actually had a rather pleasant conversation during dinner, discussing movies they'd seen in common, problems with money, life things. The physical attraction he felt toward her was hard enough to resist, but it scared him to discover they could actually talk to each other, too. He looked at the clock on the kitchen wall, reading 10:45. When he returned to the living room, the lights were out and Phil Collins played on the CD player, a soft silky sound. It was, in fact, the very CD Jake had found to be the most effective whenever he had a woman over, and now Kelly was using it.

"Don't tell me I blew another light bulb," he said, turning a lamp on at the end of the couch where Kelly sat.

"Oh, don't turn it on," she protested. "It was too bright in here. Moonlight is much nicer, don't you think?"

He went to the CD player and hit the eject button. "I hate Phil Collins," he said. "I had that CD lying around only because somebody brought it over to tape it and forgot to take it with them."

"You should listen to his songs, Jake," Kelly
said, refusing to give up. "He's a man who isn't
afraid to show his feelings." She patted the couch
next to her. "Come sit down. I'll help you get in
touch with your feelings," adding, "if you know
what I mean."

He wondered if she was a virgin. He doubted
she was, but the thought intrigued him. She had her
legs tucked up beneath her, her short skirt riding up
her smooth thighs, the material flimsy and almost
see-through, a very sexy dress which he knew she'd
bought just for the occasion. The kind of dress he'd
never be able to afford to buy her. He sat down at
the far end of the couch, but she quickly slid over,
practically lying down in his lap.

"Kelly," he said. "Can't you understand how
wrong this is? How wrong I am for you? You can't,
can you?"

"I understand more than you think, Jake," she
said softly. He knew she was telling the truth. "I know
how it feels to be alone, and to feel like the whole
world is against you. I know how difficult it can be to
share what's inside you. That's why I'm here, Jake.
Isn't it? Isn't that why, deep down, you invited me?"
She looked up at him, her enormous brown eyes pouring themselves into him. "You know how I feel, Jake,
don't you? Or do I have to say it again?"

At that moment, a knock came on the door.
Jake took one last look at Kelly in the moonlight
and then went to answer it. At the door was a
woman in her late twenties, in a black leather mini-

skirt and jacket unzipped nearly to the navel, with nothing on underneath it—busty and cover-girl gorgeous, with a head of flaming red hair that made the burning bush look like a Bic Clic. She had a bottle of champagne in her hands.

"I'm sorry I'm late, babycakes," she said to Jake. "Traffic was a bitch all the way from the marina." Jake let the woman in, his look dumbstruck.

Kelly appeared equally shocked, sitting up on the couch and covering her legs.

The redhead saw her, the smile leaving her face. "What's the deal, Jake?" the woman asked. "Who's your friend?"

"Margot," Jake said, "this is Kelly. Kelly, this is, uh, Margot." Margot smiled at Kelly, bemused.

"Hello Kelly," she said condescendingly. "Do your parents live in the building?"

"No, actually," Jake said. "Kelly and I just finished dinner."

"Wait a minute," the redhead said, her voice rising a notch. "Let me get this straight. Did we or did we not have a date tonight?"

"Margot, I'm sorry—I must have screwed up—" Jake began.

"Screwed up?" she said, getting angry. "You son of a bitch. I blew off a premiere in Westwood to see you, and the whole damn cast was going to be there. And you knew it, too."

Voices tended to carry across the courtyard at Melrose Place, so Jake moved to close the door, but Margot blocked his way.

"Margot . . ."

"You really don't give a damn, do you?" Margot said coldly. "Like we're all just a bunch of bimbos, lined up to wait our turns? What am I, Jake, Tuesday? Is that how you think of me? Well the hell with you, pal!" She made for the door.

"Margot, I'm sorry," Jake said lamely. "What else can I say?" Margot sized him up, then shrugged, tucking the champagne back under her arm.

"Forget it, Jake," she said. "You're not worth the grief." She turned to Kelly. "He's not worth it at all."

The woman stormed out the door. Jake went after her, trying to calm her down or make things all right again. When they got outside, Margot stopped and turned to Jake, smiling.

"How'd I do?" she whispered. "Did I read my lines right?"

"Right on the money," he said.

"You owe me twenty bucks for the champagne," she said. "Nice touch, don't you think? Actually," she said, looking in through the window at Kelly, who sat on the couch, devastated, "you owe me a lot more than that." Jake nodded and squeezed her arms.

When Margot was gone, Jake returned to Kelly. The deed was done, the harsh medicine administered.

"She's an old friend," he said. Kelly was on the verge of tears, and not just one of those short cries that make you feel better afterward. This was serious heartache. He'd seen it before.

"Why'd you invite her over," Kelly asked in a barely audible whisper.

"I guess it just slipped my mind," he said.

"Am I so unimportant to you that it just slipped your mind?"

"Kelly. This is who I am. This is me. This is what I do and how I live."

"Why are you treating me like this?" she wanted to know. The tears were pouring copiously down her cheeks now.

He steeled himself as he prepared to deliver the coup de grâce. "Because I feel nothing," he said. "For you, or for anyone."

She sat on the couch another few seconds, then got to her feet, walked to the counter, picked up her purse and headed for the door. She didn't look back, putting one foot in front of the other until she got to the edge of the pool. Jake was in the doorway when Kelly turned to face him.

"Okay, Jake," she said. "I'll get out of your life. For what it's worth though, I loved you. I really did."

He knew. If he knew anything at all, he knew that. He also knew that the chances were slim he'd ever find anybody who would love him again as much as Kelly had loved him, and that such a love is an incredibly valuable thing to have, something you hang onto with all your might. He also knew, though, that he'd done the right thing. Maybe in the wrong way, but maybe in the only way. He'd prevented a nice girl from ruining her life. Somehow, though, he didn't feel terribly proud of himself for doing it.

13

THE COURTYARD AT MELROSE PLACE WAS empty, the pool's surface still and mirror smooth, the underwater lights throwing up an almost eerie glow. The sky was unusually starry for Los Angeles, and there were those who said several star-filled clear-aired smogless nights in a row was a sign of an impending earthquake. It couldn't come soon enough for Jane, whose world was falling apart anyway. She'd heard of powerful earthquakes, but never one so strong it shook the wedding bands off people's fingers. She wasn't really trying to think up credible lies anyway. Rhonda and Alex had lingered by the car, exchanging meaningful glances and even more meaningful telephone numbers. Rhonda had apologized to Jane in the car for pushing her to come along, but Jane knew she had nobody to blame but herself for what had happened. Peter had said he wanted to walk Jane to her door, and she didn't mind, now that he understood the situation. He said he'd check with his bouncer friend at the club in the morning, maybe the ring would turn up. Jane could only smile and nod.

"I'd better be getting inside," she said. "I'm sure Michael is waiting up for me."

"You know," Peter said, "he might not even notice. Guys can be pretty unperceptive sometimes."

"It doesn't matter," Jane said. "I'm going to tell him the truth. You do that when you're married to someone."

"Not in most of the marriages I know," Peter said. "Only in the good ones. So what's the truth?"

"That I thought I was missing something," Jane said. "The excitement. A taste of the unknown. All of which is waiting for me behind that door over there."

"You really love him, don't you?" Peter said wistfully. " 'Oh what a lucky man he was . . .' "

"Shelley?"

"Emerson," Peter said, "Lake and Palmer."

"Thanks for the drinks and the dance," Jane said. "It really was fun, all things considered. You really are a nice guy."

"Yeah, well," Peter replied, "you know where we finish."

The apartment was dark when she entered it, with only a light on in the kitchen, where she found a half empty bottle of scotch and an empty Flintstones jelly glass, the glass Michael like to drink from when he was blue. "It cheers me up," he'd once told her, "to think I wasn't born twenty thousand years ago with a bad job and a car with a hole in the floor."

For a moment, she thought the worst, that he'd already found out somehow about the missing ring. Then she saw him, standing in the bedroom door. He looked awful.

"I've been waiting for you," he said.

"I know," Jane said. "I'm sorry."

"Where've you been?" he asked. "I feel like I've been waiting for you forever."

"I went to Shooters," Jane said, taking a deep breath. "I did something crazy without thinking—"

Before she could make her confession, Michael came to her and put his hand over her mouth. Something was wrong. When he kissed her, she felt as if she was rescuing a drowning man.

He led her by the hand to the bedroom, where every candle they owned glowed warmly in the darkness. "Don't Wait That Long" came softly from a tape player on the dresser. Jane was overwhelmed, and was about to say as much to Michael when he again put his finger to her lips, after which he slipped her jacket from her shoulders, draping it across the back of a chair.

For what he wanted to say, there were no words. He picked her up and carried her to the bed, kissing her passionately as he laid her down, unzipping her dress with his left hand. They made love, and they took their time, and the phone didn't ring, and no one knocked at the door, and when the earth moved, it was not an earthquake that was responsible, though the stars in the sky did play a small part.

Upstairs, Alison thought she smelled something burning. She threw on a robe and stepped out onto the balcony, to see, flames coming from the barbecue grill and, silhouetted in the flickering orange light, Billy, looking like a warlock performing a demonic ritual. If he was, in fact, a warlock who performed demonic rituals, she decided she would have to ask him to move out, but when she came down to join him, she saw that he was simply destroying his screenplay, one page at a time, burning the work he'd been so pleased with.

"Billy," she said. "What are you doing? It's one in the morning. You're burning your screenplay?"

"What's left of it," he said. "I told you it was going to be a hot property. Got any marshmallows?"

"Billy, this is crazy," she said. But, before she could stop him, he committed the last few pages to the flames.

"I've always been a sucker for Viking funerals," he said, watching the paper turn black, curling in on itself. When pieces of ash rose in the heat, he knocked them back down with a spatula. "You were right, Alison. I read it again. It blew chunks. I admit it and I can deal with it. But at least I managed to accomplish one thing."

"What's that?" she asked.

"I got my first flop out of the way."

"A red-letter day in any writer's life," she agreed as she watched the flames flicker.

"I can accept failure," he said. "I won't accept defeat. No way am I giving up. My head is just exploding with ideas. If I don't get them out, and lock them up on paper, it'll just make me crazy anyway. But geez, you know, I was thinking, what the fat do I know about private detectives? Next time I'm going to write about something I know."

"From the heart," Alison added.

"Exactly," he said. "Maybe something about a slacker from the Valley whose father wants him to pitch sofa sleepers on television, but the guy has dreams of his own that he refuses to give up on, so he sets off into the world with nothing but a Barca-Lounger and a word processor."

"Sounds like a good place to start."

"And Alison?"

"Hmmm?"

"You make a kick-ass tuna casserole. Is there any left?"

At Shooters, Delia was totaling the registers and ringing in the charges. Charlie, the bus boy, was sweeping up and emptying ashtrays into a large gray plastic trash can. Sandy had wiped down the tables and put the chairs up, but couldn't cash out until Delia was finished. She was shooting a game of pool while she waited when Jake walked in, looking like he'd just finished a long ride.

"Well, well," Sandy said. "The Iceman cometh. So dish, Jake. How'd your little dinner party go tonight?"

"It went," he said, picking up a cue and taking a shot, finessing the fourteen ball into the side pocket. "I scared her out of my life and broke her heart into maybe a couple thousand pieces." He shot again, missing on the twelve.

"You ought to be used to it by now, Jake," Sandy said, drawing a bead on the three ball. "When you dumped me, you bled a little bit, but you healed up quick enough." After her shot, she noticed that Jake was lost in thought and seemed, to her surprise, to be truly hurting, looking like a lost little boy. She walked around the table and put her arm around him. "You did the right thing, you know. She was a baby. Anything else and you just would have gotten in deeper. You spared her more heartache in the long run."

"I'm a regular saint, ain't I?" Jake askedd.

"You're not as selfish as you think," Sandy said. "Or as selfish as people think. Just between you and me, neither am I, but if you tell anybody I'll kill you."

Jake lined up a shot and intentionally sunk the eight ball to lose the game. "She's the only person who ever made me feel good about myself," he said.

If he'd really been listening, Sandy thought, he'd realize that that was exactly what she'd been trying to do, but his mind was obviously on other things. "You don't have a baboon's heart after all," Sandy said. "You just act like a baboon sometimes."

"Hey, Sandy," the bus boy called to her from across the room. "Come here a second."

"Charlie," she said, "can't you see we're in the middle of a game here? I'm kicking Jake's behind."

"I found something in the trash you gotta see," Charlie said, holding out his hands.

One candle in the Mancini bedroom had already spluttered out, and the rest were getting low. Immediately after she and Michael had made love, Jane had felt an overpowering glow, as if she were being slowly submerged in warm honey, and sleep would have come easily, had she chosen to sleep. But she still had something to tell Michael, so she stayed awake, waiting only a few minutes for the world and its realities to return. From his irregular breathing, she could tell Michael was awake as well, both of them lying in each other's arms.

"That was incredible," she said at last. "That was better than the first time when we moved to L.A."

He hugged her tighter. "I've never missed anyone in my life as much as I missed you tonight," he said.

"Michael, something happened," she said, mustering her courage. Her ring finger felt conspicuously bare. "There's something I want you to know."

"I lost my first patient," he said, not hearing her. "The old man with the coronary, the one who cursed me in Italian all week. He was such a crabby old fart his own family wouldn't visit him, but then, just before he went under, he grabbed my hand and said, *'per favore, non mi lasciare.'* Please, don't leave me. I promised him I wouldn't." Jane could hear Michael's voice breaking.

"Michael—"

"I know I'm not supposed to feel responsible, and just keep my distance and avoid getting emotionally involved," he said. "But Jane, how can I? That's why I wanted to be a doctor in the first place, because I care about making people . . ." He was unable to finish his thought, breaking down and sobbing silently while Jane held him and stroked his hair, saying soothing things, telling him she would always be there for him.

He was an incredibly strong man, and part of his strength was this, his tremendous compassion. Some people made fun of the new sensitive male, but Jane wouldn't trade Michael for anyone in the world. To think that he loved her more than he loved his work was nearly overwhelming to her.

They had lain still for a few minutes when Jane heard a knock at the door. She rose from bed to answer it, figuring that at this late hour, it had to be something important. When she opened it, she saw Sandy.

"Sorry to bother you so late, but I saw the kitchen light on," Sandy said. "I've got something that I think belongs to you." Michael appeared at Jane's shoulder just as Sandy handed over her wedding band. Jane's mouth dropped open. "Well it is yours, isn't it?"

In a daze, Jane slipped it on her finger. Jane

locked eyes with Sandy, pleading with her not to say anything. One day, Jane resolved, she would still tell Michael what had happened, but now was not the moment.

"I found Janie's ring in the laundry room," Sandy said to Michael, looking quickly at Jane to tell her her secret was safe.

"Thank you," Jane said.

"What are friends for?" Sandy said. "Besides, what use do I have for it?"

Sandy backed away, waving good night. After the Mancinis closed the door, she paused for a moment by the pool and looked up at the sky. She felt the way she usually felt when she looked up at the sky. Lonely. By now loneliness was like an old friend, but she had to wonder how much longer she could tell herself she could live without love and like it.

People need to know how to fool themselves, she thought, there's no other way to make it through the day. When she believed it, her life went smoothly, but she didn't always believe it. The thing was, she didn't crave love the way some people craved it, longing to have someone to take care of them or stroke them when they needed stroking. Sandy didn't long to receive love. She longed to give it. She'd just done a nice thing, and she felt proud of herself for it. Of course, doing too many nice things, in any random general sort of way, would be bad for her image. One person. It would be nice, she thought, to be nice to one person.

She was climbing the stairs when Jake entered the courtyard. She stopped.

"So?" he asked her. "Did Michael find out about the ring?"

"There was nothing to find out," Sandy said. "Jane forgot it in the laundry room, and I found it this morning and just got around to returning it. No problemo, Jake."

He smiled. "Well, my God," he said, looking at her. "I guess you're developing a conscience, too."

"We're just a couple of late bloomers, aren't we Jake?"

"If you say so," he said. For a long and awkward moment, they looked at each other. They had a great deal in common, which was what attracted them to each other and at the same time frightened them. When they'd broken up the first time, it was because they had both come to understand what a relationship between them could become—something awesome, overpowering, self-negating, explosive and destructive, eternal and impossible and magnificent. As soon as they'd known this, they'd backed away from it. But it was still there, like a sleeping giant, waiting to be awakened. They looked at each other.

"'Night, Jake," she said.

"Good night Sandy," he said, not looking away. She took a step up, but only one, waiting for the words to come. Waiting.

Coming in January

BASED ON THE HIT TV SERIES CREATED BY
DARREN STAR

MELROSE PLACE
© Spelling Television Inc.

KEEPING THE FAITH

A NOVELIZATION BY DEAN JAMES
BASED ON TELEPLAYS BY AMY SPIES,
ELLEN HERMAN, AND TONI GRAPHIA

Eight people, living and learning together . . . reaching for their dreams. Melrose Place . . . where friendship is the rule of the day.

MORNING IN LOS ANGELES MEANS MANY
things to many people. For some, it's a "window of
habitability," when the air has the illusion of clarity,
and the Angelenos are actually friendly and might
even wave hello to each other as they pick up their
morning newspapers. Then the morning commute
turns them into seething cauldrons and the air fills
with a filthy white haze, and another day begins.

For Jane and Michael Mancini, morning was
sometimes a time to be alone with each other, and
other times a time to go jogging. Neither of them
was sure which was more important to their marriage. Before they were married, they'd each exer-
cised, in no small part to stay fit and trim and

attractive to the opposite sex. Now that they were married, the point of exercising became more obscure and abstract, just part of a general "wellness" policy. All they knew for sure was that Jane had gained three pounds since her wedding day, Michael seven. He'd also told her, reading from one of his medical journals, that only a small percentage of the married population is able to maintain their wedding-day weights. They were determined not to let themselves go to pot, so to speak, and so, this morning, had decided to jog rather than spend time at home. Michael had suggested wearing ankle and wrist weights around the house to enhance the calorie burn. Jane was going to make a wisecrack about how sometimes overcoming Michael's resistance was enough of an isometric exercise, but decided to hold her tongue.

Jake Hanson had chosen this morning to work on his motorcycle, which he'd wheeled into the courtyard and parked in front of his apartment, by the pool, only because he needed to run an extension cord to power his tools. It was a 1969 Triumph 950 that he'd bought off a rich college kid whose parents cut off his spending money after he failed every class he had taken that semester. The kid was stupid in a number of other ways. He'd tricked out the bike with cheap cosmetics, a lame-looking faring, saddle bags, a touring seat, and a stereo, all items Jake had removed upon taking ownership. His first task had been to restore the bike to it's pristine condition, then second, to make it run better than it was ever designed to run. He'd completely rebuilt the engine, bored out the pistons, added racing carbs, a better suspension, new brakes, and then he'd rechromed and repainted—it was a beautiful motorcycle, "maybe not as pretty as the kind of sculpture you find in an art museum," Jake liked to say, "but a whole lot faster."

He was just finishing the muffler job when Sandy Harling appeared on her balcony, wearing her bathrobe and eating grapes. Sandy would look good wearing a packing crate, Jake thought as he looked up at her. Some women looked frumpy in bathrobes. Sandy looked the opposite, like Marilyn Monroe stepping out of her trailer on the set. She was offering a play by play of the action.

"He wipes," she called out, "he strokes, he..."

"I'm just replacing some old pipes, Sandy," he told her. "After that, I'm going to put on a new henway and then I'm done."

"What's a henway?" she asked.

"Oh, about five pounds," he replied. Rather than smile at him, she sneered. She had a beautiful sneer.

"You treat that bike better than you do most people," she said with disgust, before heading back to her own apartment.

"You're right, I do," he called after her, then muttering to himself, "for one thing, it's got more heart than most people. It never presents me with a problem I can't fix. It stays the same every day and never changes its mind. It never lies to me..." His musings were interrupted when he saw Jane and Michael race into the courtyard, finished with their morning jog.

"I won!" Jane shouted, touching the mailboxes.

"No way, Janie! I got here first," Michael said, pulling her away by the waist. She laughed and gave him an elbow, then paused to catch her breath, standing bent over with her hands on her knees. Michael's eyes rested on Jake and sauntered over, still panting. His expression suddenly turned grumpy.

"Jake," he said, "you're getting oil spots all over the tiles."

"Mornin' to you too, Michael," Jake said, nodding to Jane. She waved, then pointed to their apartment to tell Michael she had to get ready for work. Michael told her he'd join her in a minute, returning his attention to Jake.

"Do you suppose you could move your bike in the garage?" he asked, touching a spot of grease with the toe of his running shoe. "And while you're at it, drop off your rent check. Mr. Kaye called." He was just doing his job as manager, but Jake overreacted, setting his wrench down angrily.

"Why don't you just tell Mr. Kaye to call me personally?"

"I'm on your side, man," Michael said. "I just don't want to see you evicted." Sometimes, he thought, it would be a whole lot easier if he were a stranger to his tenants, instead of their friend, but then, as Jane was wont to remind him, "you catch more flies with honey . . ." Who wanted to catch flies though?

"Look—I've been busting my ass to find something," Jake said, "but it's dead in construction these days. I've got people who owe me money, but I'm having trouble getting them to pay me."

"Mr. Kaye's words exactly," Michael said. "I know it's tough..."

"Don't worry about it," Jake said. "I'll have work by the end of the day." Michael let it go, though judging by the pessimistic look on Jake's face, he wasn't sure how much of that was wishful thinking. He'd yet to evict anybody. He didn't want to start with Jake.

Alison Parker's day as receptionist at D&D Advertising had begun the way it usually did, with polite callers asking polite questions, clients trying to reach their account executives, an occasional spouse reminding a husband or wife to pick up a child or pet at a school or clinic. As the day wore on, the callers would get more insistent and crabby. After three o'clock, the worst phase would come, people from New York and/or the East Coast who'd been waiting for the rates to go down to call, usually voicing complaints and/or airing New York City attitudes. She tried to stay pleasant throughout.

"D & D Advertising," she said, trying to put a friendly tone in her voice. "Oh, hello, Mr. Danworth. Ms. Cabot won't be in 'til ten." Danworth was the vice-president in charge of one of D&D Advertising's major accounts. She still felt uneasy about sucking up to the bosses, though everyone assured her it was not only necessary but expected. The idea of a business as a form of benevolent meritocracy was naive, they all told her. She wanted to get ahead on her talent and skills, she told herself. Her sycophantry needed work. "By the way . . . congratulations on the stock split. I saw it in the *Wall Street Journal*, page three . . ." The pause on other end of the line made her wonder if she'd been overly familiar. She'd wanted only to leave him asking, "what's this—a receptionist who reads the *Wall Street Journal*?" All you could do was try.

She'd just hung up the phone when she glanced up to see Rick, an entry-level peon like herself. He worked in the mail room, was about her age, cute in a rumpled sort of way, usually clad in running shoes, blue jeans, Oxford shirts and neckties loud enough to excite the mating instincts of a South American parrot. He was leaning on her desk, smiling.

"I heard the whole thing," he said. "You were perfect. Professional but personal. Open your reward." He handed her an interoffice envelope with something bulky inside it. Curious, she took it from him.

"I was worried I overdid it," she said. He was attracted to her, she knew, and she was attracted back. In the envelope, she found a donut.

"That's not just any donut," he told her. "It's the double-dipped honey-glaze from L.A. Eats. Those things sell, used, for two and three hundred dollars, and that one is brand new this morning." She stuck her finger through the hole. Rick was funny and charming, and the best thing about him was, he didn't try too hard.

"Yesterday it was a Zen muffin, Friday it was a Mrs. Gooch's granola bar," she said. "So I'm asking myself, A: you really like the way I answer the phones, or, B: you're psychic and know I'm in major need of a sugar rush when I get to work." He only smiled at her, wheeling his mail cart down the hall.

"Don't forget possibility C," he said over his shoulder.

"Which is?" she asked. He coyly refused to answer, instead wagging his eyebrows at her. It meant he would tell her later. She was looking forward to his return visit.

Alison had once told Jake she knew of an opening in the mail room, but at the time, he'd ignored her. He had a problem with real jobs. With authority. In fact, saying Jake Hanson had a problem with authority was like saying the United States had a problem with Iraq. It made things difficult whenever Jake went to a job interview. He had little difficulty coming off as somebody who needed money—he could be very sincere and convincing about that— but it was hard to feign the proper respect for the interviewer sometimes, especially when the interviewer had only gained his or her position of authority by kissing butt and passing the buck long enough to rise to his or her level of incompetence, after which it becomes their job to quash all challenges to their position and hire only people they don't feel threatened by. It was nerdy high school crap, and it made Jake bristle. He was threatening when he was bristled. It was one reason he worked construction. He found it easy to respect men who could build things, good strong things that had a useful function and lasted. Those kind of men hired him.

The other kind, he had problems with, and he suspected, entering the Café Ami with the want-ads section of the paper under his arm, that Kurt, the manager, was going to be the kind he had problems with. Kurt was about 40, six foot and maybe 150 lbs, 160 if you included the size of his ego. When Jake asked to speak to the manager, Kurt said imperiously, "Yes?"

"I saw your help wanted ad," Jake said. "I wondered what you were looking for."

"I'll tell you what I'm not looking for," Kurt said. "Someone who's got a second career. An actor, a writer, a model. Though I suppose it's too much to ask, hoping to find someone who actually wants to be in food service. In Europe, it's an honorable profession."

"Don't worry, man," Jake said. "I work with my hands." Alison had warned him not to call people "man" in job interviews, but he'd temporarily forgotten. He held out his hands, which were still slightly soiled from working on the bike, to prove his assertion.

"Hopefully, you wash them sometimes."

"Just tell me if there's a job, okay?," he said, annoyed at the man's tone. Kurt paused to consider, looking Jake up and down.

"You do have the right look," he said. He led Jake behind the bar and motioned to a cappuccino machine that reminded Jake of a 1952 Vincent Black Lightning. "Have you ever worked one of these?" Jake shook his head. Kurt removed the filter, knocked out the espresso grounds and proceeded to demonstrate the machine. "Have you even had a cappuccino?"

"I had one when I was a little kid but it ran away," Jake said. "It's a kind of monkey, right?" Kurt stared at him blankly. Obviously, he had no sense of humor. It was good to find that out right away, Jake thought.

"Watch carefully," Kurt continued. "The right dose can be ruined by poor tamping, but harder tamping prevents watery espresso. Just try to remember, you're not grinding cement. Do you think you can handle it?"

"No problem," Jake said. "It's a glorified Mr. Coffee."

"Mr. Coffee can't make macchiato." Kurt scowled. "People do not drive from all over L.A. for Mr. Coffee."

Jake quickly, easily and correctly copied the motions Kurt had just shown him. He'd once taken apart a lawn mower engine when he was seven and successfully reassembled it, "a freakin' Mozart around machinery," his father had praised him. The cappuccino machine was not going to be the problem with this job. Kurt was.

Alison had asked Rick to join her for lunch, brown bags on the lawn outside D&D, under the shade of a tall oak tree. His lunch was a sandwich from the cafeteria, hers an assortment she'd packed that morning. Rick took an interest in her food.

"I'll bet you carried a Star Wars lunch box to school," he said. He was right, but she wasn't about to admit it. Princess Leia, before the Hollywood scene got to her. "You can tell a lot about people from how they pack their lunches."

"Like what?"

He picked up a celery stalk, holding it up for her perusal. "The perfect but generous use of peanut butter tells me you love peanut butter and are benignly compulsive," he said. He held up her Tupperware container. "You're ecologically aware, and," he said, holding up her grapes, "unnecessarily diet-conscious." She licked the peanut butter from her celery stalk.

"I figured after those high carbo snacks you've been giving me, I'd go light on lunch," she said with a grin. Across the lawn, Alison spotted a woman getting into her Alfa Romeo convertible, an attractive woman in her early thirties, today in an Armani suit and Charles Jourdan high heels, no doubt heading to some swank upscale restaurant for a hundred-dollar business lunch, talking animatedly with a man in a navy blue blazer. Rick followed Alison's gaze.

"Lucy Cabot," he said, dropping grapes into her napkin.

"I know," Alison said. "VP on Sun Ray Sunscreen. God, she's so confident. It's like she could walk through a brick wall. Sometimes I wonder if that will be me in ten years."

"She's a major chocoholic. You can soften her with Hershey bars," Rick said.

"What are you, the mail room snoop?" As Lucy Cabot drove past, she waved at Rick. He waved back. Alison was shocked. "She knows you?"

"Yeah," he said. "I'd rather not get into it."

"C'mon, I'm curious," Alison said. For a moment, she wondered if there'd been some sort of romantic connection.

"Promise you won't tell anyone at work?" She nodded. "My last name is Danworth. As in the son of Joe Danworth."

"Our sunscreen account," she said. "I put through a call from your father this morning."

"Well if you're impressed, don't be," Rick said with a frown. "You have no idea what a drag it is having a heavy-hitter for a father."

"It beats having zero connections," Alison said, packing up the Tupperware.

"It's a burden, actually," Rick apprised her. "Why do you think I get to work at six every day? Sometimes I feel I have to work twice as hard just to prove myself."

"God," she said, sympathizing. "And I thought connections were supposed to get you somewhere."

Rick rose and then helped her to her feet. She took his hand. She always remembered the first physical contact she had with men. For some reason though, she never remembered the last. Alison shook her head at the thought as Rick brushed the new mown grass from his pants, ran his fingers through his hair, then straightened his tie and smiled at her.

"So, listen, how about dinner tonight?" he said.

The only sign of nervousness was the rocking of his feet as he waited for an answer.

"I beg your pardon," she joked. "I just met you a few days ago."

"What are you gonna do that's better—go home and rent a video?" He leaned toward her, anxious to hear her response.

"Okay, okay," she said, pretending to be giving in. "But you know what they say about romance in the work place."

"Tell me."

"Risky business," she cautioned. "Oprah did a whole show on office rendezvous spots. Elevators, supply closets..."

"I like it, I like it," Rick said, opening the door for her. "I want to hear every one of them . . ."

The lunch rush at Café Ami was well under way by the time Alison was back at her desk. The crowd was comprised, for the most part, of business executives on expense accounts, which was probably why the place could get away with charging five dollars for a blueberry muffin, Jake thought. From what he could overhear, there were advertising big shots talking about demographics, movie people discussing pitches and concepts and development packages, and in one corner, Jake saw one of the actresses from the old "Cosby Show," though she'd only wanted hot water, having brought her own herbal tea which she carried in a leather sack as if it contained precious gems. Everyone else was having some form of coffee, and

Jake was swamped. Kurt had only hired him because he knew they'd be swamped and were short-handed. Kurt stood over Jake like a mother hen, fussing and making everything just that much more difficult.

"Rusty on our calculus, are we?" Kurt said. "The pitcher has to be one third full. One third. That's one half."

"I got it under control," Jake said, grabbing the cinnamon.

"And shake the cinnamon gingerly," Kurt said.

"We mixing metaphors or spices?" Jake said.

"Just remember," Kurt huffed, "you're not hammering nails anymore. Thusly and so forth," he said, taking the cinnamon from Jake's hand and demonstrating it again. Jake wished he had a hammer in his hand right then, but only to nail Kurt to the wall, somewhere out of the way where he wouldn't bother people.

"I'm overdue for a break," Jake reminded his boss.

"We're way too busy," Kurt said. "That group gets a mocha, a macciato, an iced latte, and a double decaf' cap."

"Whatever happened to plain old coffee?" Jake muttered under his breath as Kurt walked away. He was finishing up the iced latte when he heard a familiar voice.

"Jake?"

He looked up to see Perry Kraft. His first reaction was to smile, which was how most people, most men anyway, reacted when they saw her. She was as sexy a woman as any he'd ever known, both

for the way she looked and for the risks she was
willing to take. She was wearing a red miniskirt
with a leopard-spotted silk blouse, opened provocatively low in front. She was the perfect combination
of good times and bad news, and he couldn't help
but glance at her hands to see how many men she
had, wrapped around her little finger. She leaned
across the bar and kissed him hello.

"Perry," Jake said hesitantly. "Long time."

"Yeah, gotta be years. I thought that was your
bike out front."

"Of all the cappuccino joints in L.A., you had
to come into this one," he said, not even trying to
sound like Bogart, which was how Bogart would
have done Bogart, if he wasn't already.

"Don't tell me you own this place," she said as
she glanced around the crowded room. "I thought
you were allergic to trendy."

"I've had my shots," he said. She had the
strangest way of making a man feel ten feet tall and
lower than a worm at the same time. "I just work
here. It's temporary." He returned to the cappuccino machine, feeling her eyes on him.

"I love the way you bury that nozzle," she said.
"You always did have the touch." He stopped what
he was doing and looked at Perry, who was clearly
trying to seduce him. He was not feeling entirely
averse to being seduced. They were interrupted when
Kurt came by to tell him they were five orders behind.

"What do you think you're doing?" Kurt said.
Jake looked the manager in the eye. Without thinking twice, Jake grabbed his jacket, stepped around

the counter and grabbed Perry by the arm.

"Coffee break," Jake said adamantly. "It's the law, Kurt. Fifteen minutes." He led Perry out of the restaurant, walking over to where his bike was parked. He felt slightly foolish at having to take any lip from Kurt in front of her.

"Tough times?" she asked.

"Depends on how you look at it."

"Remember when we drove to the desert and made love in the middle of the road on this bike?," she said, running her finger along the handlebar.

"It was a nice ride," Jake said, remembering. "The bike held up pretty good."

"So did you," she said. Jake pointed to the take-out bag Perry was holding.

"So, who's the lucky guy?"

"Clients," she said with a believe-it-or-not air. She laughed at some private joke. "I'm an art dealer these days."

"What?" he said. "You don't know anything about art."

"That's the great thing about L.A. All you need is the right look."

"You've always had the right look," he told her.

She smiled wickedly. "You look like you could use some action. I've got something going that could make us both a lot of money." She was fishing for him, luring him in the way she used to. He was falling for it, the way he used to.

"No, thanks. I'm doin' fine on my own."

"Jake, it's legit.'"

"I'm not sure your idea of legit' and mine are

the same," he told her. She was unblinking, looking at him the way a cat watches its prey before attacking, waiting for a sign of weakness. She took a step toward him, then grabbed him by the arm and rolled up his sleeve. She took the pen out of his breast pocket and wrote her telephone number on his wrist.

"My calzones are getting cold," she said. "Call me."

"We wouldn't want your calzones to freeze," he said. "Get out of my life, will you Perry?"

"Break's over!" Kurt shouted out the kitchen door. "So's your job if you pull this stuff again!" Perry looked at Kurt, then at Jake.

"And what a life it is, too," she said sarcastically. She strolled to her car, a black convertible, and looked at him one last time before driving away. He read the number on his arm. Operator, get me trouble, he thought. With a capital "T." Before he went back to work, he copied the number onto a piece of paper, so that he wouldn't lose it.

Rhonda Blair was looking through her mail in the vestibule when she saw Matt Fielding locking his car. He looked as if he'd spent the day pushing rocks up the other side of Sysyphus's mountain, tired and bedraggled with his tie loosened and off to the side. He worked as hard as any man she knew, at a job that was often thankless, running a shelter for runaway kids. Rhonda was tired in her own way, having taught a late aerobics class that had worn her out. She greeted her friend with a smile.

"I never figured my most ongoing adult relationship would be with the utility companies," she
said, not even attempting to conceal her disgust.
"Look at all these bills. If I'm going to pay this
much for electricity I might as well buy the Hoover
Dam. It's got to be Sandy's hair drier."

"Rhonda, spare me," Matt said tiredly. She
gathered he'd had a hard day, and asked what was
wrong. "Work stuff," he replied. "Actually, reality
stuff. More funding got cut from my halfway house.
We had to let our head cook go."

"Wow. So what are you going to do?"

"I have this pool of potential volunteers," he
told her, "but it's tough pulling people away from
paying jobs these days."

"Hey, let me help tomorrow night," Rhonda
said. "I bet your kids would love my chicken curry."
Matt looked at her skeptically. She was always full
of enthusiasm and vigor, but it had been his experience that such enthusiasm was likely to wane with
time, and not much time at that.

"Are you sure? If you are, I'll stop looking for
someone else."

"No problem, I'm gonna be there," she said. "I
swear." She kissed him on the cheek and then ran
up the stairs to her apartment, where she found the
door ajar. She was almost knocked over by Sandy as
she entered the hallway. Sandy was carrying spiked
heels and a funky black dress.

"Alison's got a hot date," Sandy said, adding
magnanimously, "I'm offering her my best 'come

and get me' dress." Rhonda accompanied her roommate to Alison's apartment, where they found
Alison standing before her bed, dressed in a robe.
On the bed were five dresses, and Alison was trying
to choose between them. Sandy threw the black
number down on top of the others.

"So what do you think, Alison?" Sandy wanted
to know. "Satisfaction guaranteed."

Alison looked at the dress. "Sandy, that's
sweet," she said skeptically. It was the kind of dress
that, back in Eau Claire, might have drawn a "tsking"
comment or raised a few eyebrows. For L.A., it was
fairly modest. "But is it me?"

"What does it matter if it does the trick?" At
that moment, Billy Campbell stuck his head in the
door, his hair wet fresh from the shower.

"Somebody doing tricks tonight?" he asked
innocently.

"Billy," Alison said, "don't you have a cab fare
to torture or a novel to pretend to write?" He
joined them, wrapped in a towel. He examined the
clothes strewn about on the bed.

"You guys are scary," he said. "It's like
you're preparing for warfare, or something.
Actually I've always thought of makeup as just
another form of war paint. Hey—I like this little
black number."

"Sweetheart," Sandy said, "they don't call it
the 'battle of the sexes' for nothing."

"What does this guy do, anyway?" he asked,
turning toward Alison.

"He works in the mail room, but his dad owns

Sun Ray Sunscreen," she said. "Not that he wants anyone to know. I think it's great, but he doesn't want to talk about it."

"If you want my advice," he said, "don't let him know you're so interested. Keep talking about business, and let him make all the moves. And ask him questions about himself, it'll make him think you're interested."

"I am interested," Alison insisted. "And besides, Sandy's the actress, not me."

The doorbell rang. Billy sprinted toward the front door before Alison could stop him. He was curious to see the kind of guy Alison would date, mostly because in all the time he'd been her roommate, she'd yet to score. At least not at home. He opened the door to see Rick, wearing jeans and a shirt, with a tie that seemed to say, please, shoot me—put me out of my misery. He gave Billy a puzzled look.

"Hi," he said awkwardly. "Is Alison here?"

Billy pointed toward Alison's bedroom. He held out his hand, and Rick took it.

"She's in there. I'm her roommate."

"Alison didn't tell me..."

"Strictly platonic, but we're very close," Billy said. "She must have mentioned me."

"Actually, I don't think so," Rick said.

"I guess you guys haven't known each other long enough," Billy said confidently. "So. You plan on taking her someplace nice?"

"Yeah, probably," Rick said.

"And what are your intentions?"

Listening from behind the door, Alison was horrified, getting dressed as quickly as possible in the dress Sandy had brought. She didn't quite fill the dress the way she'd seen Sandy fill it, and she didn't have Sandy's legs, but then that was good, she thought, that would look pretty strange, walking around with four legs. Billy was making her punchy.

"God help me," she said. "Billy's in there and he's decided to protect me."

"I think it's sweet," Sandy said. Rhonda was at the door, watching Billy and trying to get a quick look at Rick.

"One-thirty at the latest," Billy was telling Rick. "I know it sounds crazy, but I do wait up."

Alison separated the two of them just in time, before Billy humiliated her even further. She greeted Rick and asked him if he'd met Billy. They shook hands again, after which Billy slapped Rick hard on the back.

"I think we understand each other, young man," Billy said.

Alison took Rick by the arm. "'Night, Dad," Alison said.

"Honey," Billy called over his shoulder to an imaginary wife, hooking his thumbs around imaginary suspenders, "fetch me my pipe and slippers. I believe I'll watch a little television. They grow up so fast, don't they?"

Rick's car was nothing to write home about, but the restaurant was, a fancy place in Venice called Solo Pasta, with corny murals of gondoliers on the walls and piped in music that sounded like it came off the soundtrack for *The Godfather*. Alison ordered medallions of veal in mushroom sauce, Rick the house lasagna, explaining that it was the true measure of any Italian restaurant, and after dinner they split a chocolate canoli for dessert. Alison initiated the post-prandial chitchat by asking him if he'd always dreamed of working in a mail room.

"Actually," he said, "I used to want to be a musician. My dad felt that more doors were open in advertising. It's true, but sometimes I feel like an alien at work."

"I know what you mean," she confessed. "But I'm finally starting to make some friends, I guess. Sometimes it just feels like high school all over again, wondering if you're popular, where you stand, who you want to sit next to in the cafeteria."

Rick made a face. "I hated high school," he said. He asked Alison how she'd chosen advertising for a profession.

"Well," she said. "I wanted to do something creative." She raised her eyebrows mockingly, to acknowledge that was she was doing now was hardly creative. "My dad was a salesman, and I always used to dream of ad lines for his products. They'd just come to me in the middle of the night. I even thought of one for your dad." She stopped herself, not wanting to sound pushy, and after all, this was pleasure, not business. "God, I'm rambling on."

"No, tell me your idea," he said, leaning toward her.

"Okay," she agreed. "Sunscreen is very nineties, environmentally aware, hole-in-the-ozone, right? It helps people, it has an ecological twist, but it's sensual. So, I was thinking of a sexy campaign like, 'It's hotter than a burn.'"

Rick thought about what she'd said for a minute, then nodded admiringly. "That's great," he said. "My dad should hear this. I mean, no pressure or anything. We'll see how things go."

Alison was immediately unsure of whether or not she should have said anything. Maybe that was what they meant about mixing business and pleasure. She didn't want Rick to think she was only using him as a conduit to his father, because she really liked him, and she hoped he knew that. Yet she couldn't help being just a little excited, to think that she was finally getting a break.

When they reached her apartment, he walked her only as far as the mailboxes, realizing, she assumed, that it was a first date and too soon to push things any further, a gentleman, even. He asked if he'd brought her home before curfew, and wondered if Billy had called the police.

Alison laughed and told him she'd had a really good time. He said he'd had an even better time. When they kissed good night, she concluded that Los Angeles men were better kissers than Wisconsin boys. She wanted to kiss Rick again, and was looking forward to her next opportunity. With a little skip in her walk, she headed for her apartment where she knew Billy was probably waiting up. Dad, indeed, she thought as she reached for the doorknob.